Tell Me Everything and Other Stories

The Katharine Bakeless Nason Literary Publication Prizes

The Bakeless Literary Publication Prizes are sponsored by the Bread Loaf Writers' Conference of Middlebury College to support the publication of first books. The manuscripts are selected through an open competition and are published by University Press of New England/Middlebury College Press.

Competition Winners in Fiction

1996
Katherine L. Hester, *Eggs for Young America*
judge: Francine Prose

1997
Joyce Hinnefeld, *Tell Me Everything and Other Stories*
judge: Joanna Scott

Tell Me Everything

and Other Stories

Joyce Hinnefeld

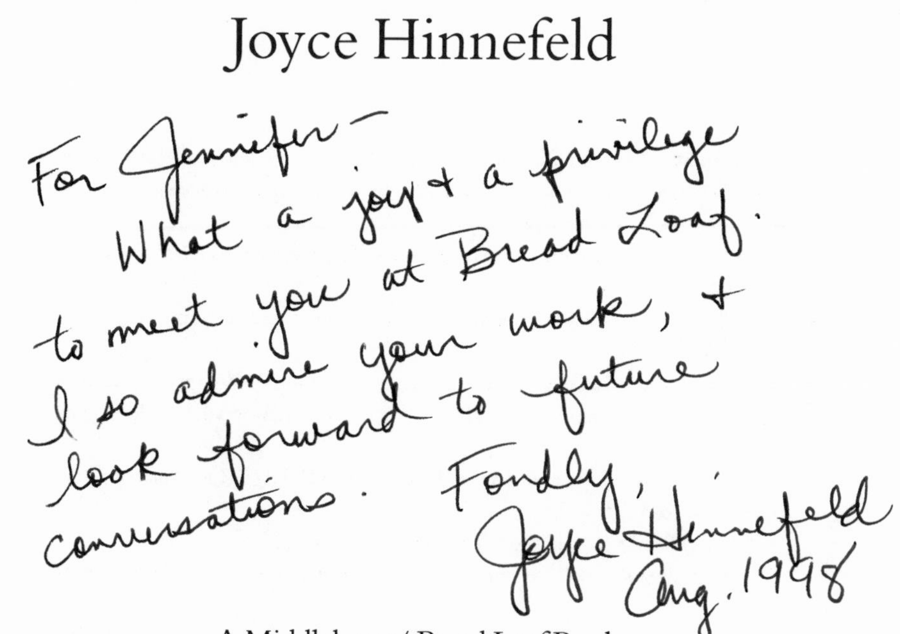

A Middlebury / Bread Loaf Book

Published by University Press of New England ~ Hanover and London

Middlebury College Press
Published by University Press of New England,
Hanover, NH 03755

Printed in the United States of America 5 4 3 2 1
CIP data appear at the end of the book

Acknowledgments

"Jump Start" was published in *13th Moon* 13 (1995) and in *Many Lights in Many Windows: Twenty Years of Great Fiction and Poetry from The Writers Community* (Milkweed Editions, 1997).

"Speaking in Tongues" was published in *Farmer's Market* 10, no. 1 (Spring/Summer 1993).

"Tell Me Everything" was published in *The Greensboro Review*, no. 59 (Winter 1995–96).

"Echo Guilt" was selected for the 1997 Community Writers Association (Providence, R.I.) Grand Prize and appeared in the CWA newsletter *Byline* (Fall 1997).

"Fallow" was published in *Prairie Hearts: Women's Writings on the Midwest* (Outrider Press, 1996).

"Fitness Tests" was published in *The Little Magazine* 19 (1993).

"What Alma Knows" was published in the Spring 1998 issue of *Room of One's Own*.

"Stories about Miranda" is adapted from a longer work and was published in the May 1998 issue of *Black Water Review*.

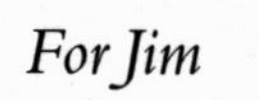
For Jim

Contents

Tell Me Everything and Other Stories

1. Unsubjected

Used to smoke marijuana every day. Gets nervous in crowds.

Walked to the YMCA today, early. Liked the just-emptied-out feeling of the place. Prefers her own neighborhood to the rows of lace-curtained brownstones near the Y. May want to live like that one day but can't see it now.

Called an old boyfriend. Hung up.

Likes these rainy days. Old, musty-smelling things. May have seen an old dress of hers on a mannequin in a second-hand shop, which would have to make it third-hand at least. Wanted a cigarette for just a minute there.

At the Y did so many laps it was hard to keep a count. Didn't count, in fact. Felt almost dizzy, even in the water.

Likes underwater invisibility best of all. Can get into a real dream state there, even at the YMCA.

Sat at her desk, head turned to the window, and lost track of the time. Nothing in the cupboard. A five-dollar bill in her purse. Contemplated registering for classes, signing up for another student loan.

Realized it was too late to swim again because of the after-work crowd at the Y.

Walked to the park. Dodged the skate boarders. Doesn't understand their haircuts or their clothing. Isn't that much older than they are.

Ate some dried apricots out of a sticky plastic bag, ignoring intent pigeons at her feet. Thought about going to a pay phone to call an old friend. Didn't do it.

Tried to get lost in some Coltrane on her walkman. Walking along blocks that fit the mood—old wood shingle two- and three-flats, peeling paint, desolate skin-and-bones men. For a second there it happened: sax riffs in her blood.

Found herself at the YMCA. Post-work crowd emptiness all around and just a clean washed chlorine smell. Nodded at the lifeguard, dove in without a shower. Hair barely dry from the last time.

Tries to find that rhythm in her strokes, to make her blood move with the quiet waves. Breathes hard and hardly notices.

At twenty-two, often thinks of sex as maybe the only redemption. Knows it is like religion—not readily available to the skeptic except in cheap imitations. Has to settle for this chlorinated baptism instead. Adjusts her goggles, dips down, blows air into water, watches what it does, goes on.

Exits ravenous for the first time in a while. Remembers leftover Chinese food in the refrigerator with lightheaded elation.

Eats all of it, ice-cold. Stares at a lettuce leaf in the kitchen sink. Can't, for the life of her, remember eating any lettuce. Sits at her desk, head turned to the window, and loses track of the time.

Dreams of a dark intruder in her room, her bed. Mumbling something indecipherable, wrapped in sheets of something, mummy-like.

Like so many mornings will wake up cold and muzzled-feeling. Will drink weak tea, leaving the bag in the kitchen sink. Will contemplate registering for classes. Will walk for hours and stare in windows. Will swim at the off-hours at the YMCA.

* * *

At some point, at the YMCA, at the twentieth, the thirtieth, the fiftieth lap, has lost any sense of "she" or "I." Has gleefully, giddily let it loose. Unsubjected, there is only her. Her blood, her strokes, her gusted air. Her sink, her desk, her bed, her past—all solid and dispensable. Easily ignored.

Her body, though, is something else. Strong, buoyant, improvised. Like jazz. Every lap a little different.

All the rest is muted, only air and water in her ears.

Jump Start

Patty gets her jump start early—coffee in the morning, instant—and she gets in her car and drives. This is all she ever wanted, maybe all she ever wanted in her life. She's like a tune you can't stop singing in the corner of your whirling mind. She's traveling down the road like an animal that's sleek to a job you might not like to do.

Patty's driving like there's no tomorrow, or lots of tomorrows, she feels that good. It's the kind of day when she can think she's alive for some kind of wild and lovely reason, her mother and father are dead from the accident but she's alive and kicking and today she can think that sure, lots of things are sad, but today she's alive and she's driving her car.

It may be that the air is crisp and cool. Feel how crisp it is. Patty likes those kinds of changes, hot to suddenly cool and fresh, and she hopes that you do, too. The accident happened when it was hot—blazing hot sun on the asphalt—and ever since then Patty hasn't cared much for the heat. Plus she can smell pine behind the trailer court and the earth looks rich and dark, not pale and dusty like some goddamn migrant camp, which is what her father would have called the trailer court. In fact he probably did call it that—how else would Patty have thought of it now?

Patty knows the other girls at the packing plant laugh at her behind her back, knows they think she doesn't know, call her "the baby" and "the kid," even Essie who barely speaks English and must not even know what those words mean. But on days when it's crisp and cool and she can smell the pine she doesn't care, she likes the drive and she's glad to see the girls again, doesn't care if they talk and click their tongues about her dead parents and what happened to her brain when she's not there because she'll be there soon enough and then they'll all just laugh on their break anyway, sit out in the cool breeze at the picnic tables and laugh and carry on.

Each day on the way to work Patty drives by the clinic at the edge of town—drives by humming today, she's still got her jump start, still can smell the pine and see the shadow leaves outside the trailer where the sun shines through the branches above her car. She can drive and drive and never lose her jump start. Patty's a fine driver—just watch her, look at how alert she is—everyone knows the accident was not her fault.

At the clinic she sees Father McElvey again with his sign that says "They're killing babies" and he waves at her and smiles and she smiles back but she's told him she won't come and hold a sign on her lunch break. And all he says is, Let me know if you change your mind.

But the girls at the plant call him fathead and el loco padre and worse, and they curse him in Spanish and laugh at him and all the people with him holding up their signs, the younger ones that the girls call "retards" and the old women with scarves tied around their heads even in the summer, even in ninety-degrees-in-the-shade summer time. Their wrinkled old fingers move fast along their rosary beads and some of them hold dusty pictures of the Virgin of Guadalupe—who has dark skin and stands on top of what looks like a snake holding a moon, Patty's noticed—up against their chests like shields.

Since the accident Father McElvey likes to come by and talk to her and he wants her to come to his church. But Patty can't slow down long enough for that—not even long enough to go and hold a sign on her lunch hour because she knows the surest way to lose her jump start would be to slow down that long, long enough to stop and think, like all that time in the hospital after the accident. And if she went and held a sign the girls would have that to laugh at about her, too. Some mornings she's seen one or two of their cars there at the clinic, Linda's maybe or Sandra's, and Patty can't make the connection between these slim girls in their tight jeans and their husky cigarette voices and the pictures of bloody babies that Father McElvey and the retards and the old women hold up in their faces when they walk out of the clinic. Because where, inside those skin-tight blue jeans, would a baby that size fit?

But Father McElvey seems like such a nice man and he smiles and nods at her and she doesn't think he would lie about the babies and those old women with their rosary beads seem like they want to cry all the time, so somebody or something must die inside there, but Patty doesn't really know what to make of it all and the girls at the packing plant aren't too much help.

"Hey Patty, don't let him sink his claws in you," Sandra said to her once. It was the day Father McElvey pulled his car up alongside the picnic tables while they ate their lunch outside and handed Patty a flier about a church potluck the following Sunday. "You start going to that man's potlucks and you'll never grow up, little girl." But I'm not a little girl! Patty wanted to say, she wanted to yell that at Sandra but she didn't say a thing. And she wondered why they all hated Father McElvey so much, what he did besides hold up the signs and the pictures of the bloody babies.

Patty wasn't Catholic though and she didn't think she ever would be. Her parents never went to church and she didn't know about her brother. He was in the army when the accident happened and now he was in Texas—he'd never come back—and after she'd stared at the dead bodies of her parents sprawled there on the highway for a while some woman she didn't know came up to her and said "I'll pray for their souls" and Patty stared at her because she didn't know what that meant, just stared at her until the hot sun made it seem like the woman was melting there in front of her, turning into something soft and rubbery right in front of Patty's eyes, and then the next thing she knew she blacked out and she never saw that woman again until one morning when she drove past the clinic on her way to the factory she saw her there next to Father McElvey with her rosary beads in one hand and a sign that said "Stop the killing" in the other one. It startled Patty to see the woman's face—it was solid now—and she heard the woman's voice all over again, heard it like it was just yesterday, heard her say "I'll pray for their souls" and still didn't know what that meant and didn't really care.

Because she'd lost her jump start for a while then. And she thought she might not want to be a Catholic after that even though Father McElvey was nice to her ever since the accident and it seemed like he always wanted to have her around.

Feel Patty's foot in her sneaker on the accelerator. Feel how she gets the pressure just right. Keeps it right there at fifty, then lifts her foot off just at the crest of the hill at the edge of town, right where the speed zone starts, lifts it off and watches the needle course back down, as smooth and gradual as the smooth hill Patty glides down, to thirty. That day last summer she'd looked down to check, to make sure she wasn't going over fifty-five so her father wouldn't yell (she'd just gotten her license, she was showing her father how careful she was, how she could drive the car just fine) and when she looked back up she saw the truck barreling right toward her face and so she swerved and he drove his giant truck right into the side of the car, right into her parents and they were covered in blood then and dead and her head was bleeding, too, but she lived.

At the bottom of the hill is the clinic and Patty is starting to lose her jump start just as she gets there so she looks for Father McElvey over in the parking lot, thinking maybe a smile from him will help her get it back though she kind of doubts it. She doesn't see Father McElvey at first—he's not in his usual place. But then she spots him and when she sees what he's doing it takes her by surprise (but she keeps her eyes on the road—she's a careful driver, it might have slowed her down in other ways but everyone agrees she's a careful driver and they all decided she should be able to keep on doing that). He's walking alongside Dorrie Lambert, a young woman Patty has always admired. Dorrie's parked her car in the clinic lot and Father McElvey is walking right beside her toward the door and a couple of the old women are with them, too, walking along with their rosaries and sticking pictures of bloody babies in Dorrie Lambert's face and they're saying things to her that must be awful, the way their faces look (though Patty can't hear their words) and Dorrie is covering her face and looking down at the ground and trying to ignore them but it's clear that Dorrie is crying.

Leave her alone!

Patty screams it inside her car but the window is up. And as she screams she swerves to the right and for a split second she can't breathe, she feels like something has hit her in the stomach but she makes herself pull the wheel back the other way, straightens out the car and slows way down but keeps on driving. And she is terrified, her heart is pounding in her ears, and she glues her eyes to the road and concentrates as hard as she can all the way to the parking lot at the plant and when she turns off the engine and steps out of her car her legs are shaky and she has to steady herself for a moment, has to hold on to the handle of the car door and catch her breath and get her heart to stop racing and her legs and hands to stop shaking, before she walks into the plant to punch the clock and go to work.

Patty's jump start is gone now, long gone, and she has too much on her mind. Usually Patty is one of the best girls on the line—she's fast and neat—but today the legs of the chickens seem to look too much like her own, their bumpy skin like the gooseflesh on her own arms that day after the accident (she remembers staring down at her right arm for the longest time, thinking how strange it was to have goose bumps, to feel so cold her teeth were chattering, there in the middle of that steaming hot highway), and even though she knows it's really just her own beating pulse that she's feeling, when she rubs her gloved fingers over their bodies, inside and out, Patty can't shake the idea that she feels these chickens' hearts beating there at the tips of her fingers. She's slowing things down and at lunchtime the supervisor asks is she all right—and he looks nervous when he asks it, like he might have been expecting this to happen, Patty thinks—and she says she's fine, she just isn't feeling quite right and he says, Why don't you take half a sick day, go on now, I'll clock out for you, so Patty has to get in her car and drive again and now it's noon and not so cool and crisp but at least the women with their signs are gone when she drives by the clinic and so is Dorrie Lambert's car and Father McElvey is nowhere in sight.

Patty thinks that's good because she's decided that the tobacco stains on his teeth when he smiles make her feel sick and she never wants to go to his potlucks or be a Catholic, which from what she can tell means being a retard or an old woman with a scarf on your head in the middle of the summer, making younger women who are prettier than you are cry.

Dorrie Lambert was a high school cheerleader when Patty was twelve and she had the best rhythm of all the high school girls by far. At halftime at basketball games when the band played songs with drums pounding out the beat and the pom-pom girls in the bleachers doing their routines, the cheerleaders stood at the sidelines doing their motions in rhythm with the drums—slap the thighs twice, clap hands, snap fingers, shake hips—and Patty and the other kids sat in the bleachers and did the motions too, wiggled their butts on the seats and clapped and shook their shoulders. Dorrie Lambert had it down better than anyone, she always had the rhythm just right; just thinking about it Patty feels the beat inside her and moves to it there on the car seat. She was always sorry when the halftime show was over.

Sometimes Patty and her friends would make up their own routines to songs on the radio in the backyard but once she stopped outside the kitchen door in time to hear her father say something about "shaking her ass like some colored girl" and when her mother clicked her tongue at him he slapped her and after that

Patty only did the dances by herself in her room with the door closed and the music turned down low. As she got older she knew better than to think she could ever be a cheerleader—it's the kind of thing you just know—and she stopped dancing by herself in front of her bedroom mirror because any time she tried she felt embarrassed.

The trailer is hot in the afternoon sun and Patty tries to sleep but she keeps waking up sweating with a picture in her mind of the old woman at the accident holding a picture of a bloody baby in Dorrie Lambert's face. Patty thinks someone who got it all so right, who moved just like that with the beat from the drums in high school shouldn't have to cry, shouldn't have to have Father McElvey and all those women mumbling awful things in her ear, even if she does have a baby inside her that she doesn't want to keep.

Patty lies sweating in her bed and she feels just like she felt after the accident, and it frightens her to feel that way again. She knows that something had better happen soon or her jump start could be gone for good. When the sun goes down at last she walks outside to the woods behind the trailer court and she can smell the pine then, smell the pine and forget about the hot, hot highway and she wishes, then, in those cool woods with a breeze on her face, that she could take Dorrie Lambert in her arms and tell her not to cry. Back in the trailer she sleeps with the window wide open and the night air blowing in and she thinks she can smell the pine trees even there in her bed and she doesn't wake up once until her alarm goes off at seven A.M. in the morning.

Patty tries to get her jump start again—has her instant coffee in the same cracked cup her mother used—but it's not working now, she can't get the feeling right, and driving along the highway she knows it's because she's mad. She's mad at Father McElvey and all those women with their scarves and fat, dry fingers. "I'll pray for their souls," she said, and Patty thinks el loco padre, yes el loco padre, hears herself scream Leave her alone! and feels that terror in her chest again as the car nearly swerves to the right one more time.

This time when she reaches the crest of the hill Patty keeps her foot on the accelerator. She can see the tips of the women's signs ("They're killing babies!") and she pictures Dorrie Lambert crying on an operating table—what if she couldn't sleep? what if she felt them cutting into her skin?—and she catches a glimpse of Father McElvey's black-coated back.

Still Patty doesn't lift her foot. She watches as the needle stays at fifty, and then it's like a dream as her foot pushes down and it moves up to sixty, seventy, eighty (where you feel it first is the ball of your foot but it moves up fast to your chest and then your throat, it's almost like you're spitting something out that you've had inside forever), and she's heading right for them, right for that goddamn Virgin of Guadalupe (Sandra's voice: "*Hey* padre—what would *you* know about Nuestra Señora de Guadalupe!" Someone has left a pile of Catholic pamphlets in the plant lounge one day and Patty knows the girls all think it was her but it wasn't).

Now Patty points her car toward the Virgin and drives like there's no tomorrow, or maybe all kinds of tomorrows. She feels that good.

Speaking in Tongues

She was named Mary, for the mother of Jesus, but her thoughts tended to run more toward Mary Magdalene. Saved from stoning by the tender son of God, she washed his feet with her tears and dried them with her long, flowing hair. It was an image Mary cherished, secretly, in a private part of her self. She saw the hair growing damp and tangled as Mary Magdalene's hand rubbed the strands lovingly over the rough skin of Jesus's feet, then limp and shining as she stroked his washed feet with thick, rich-smelling oil. Tears and oil blending in narrow streams on his skin; the love she felt for him, the things that poured from her.

Mary was sixteen that summer. She lived with her father, a farmer, and her mother, a teacher, in Kosciusko County, a tiny corner in northeastern Indiana. A place where Amish men drove horse-drawn buggies next to pick-up trucks driven by young men in seed company caps, their ruddy faces framed by loaded rifles stacked in gun racks hung behind their heads. A place where most people, non-Amish included, went to church at least twice a week, praying for the plight of the world, but mostly for the desperate plight of the seeds they planted each spring and fall.

She and her parents were not Amish, but she had learned from her father a deep and abiding admiration for the Amish way of life—simpler, purer in his eyes, related, faintly, to a distant memory of the life of his grandfather. She did not, like some of her high school classmates, laugh at the girls her age in long dresses and bonnets, the boys struggling against the heavy soil with wooden plows caked with mud.

She was sixteen, and she was happy that it was summer, happy for the relief of it. Not so much from her studies (though she worked hard, trying for a scholarship; her parents wanted her to go to college, to become a teacher like her mother). It was more of a relief to be free of the social pressures. She wasn't dating much. Boys made her nervous. She thought of them, alternately, as foolish and as hopelessly out of her reach.

"You're too choosy," her mother said to her one day early in the summer. A boy named Peter had asked Mary to a movie, and Mary had declined.

"You're being too choosy, and it's going to hurt you in the long run. Eventually boys are going to stop asking you out altogether because they're going to start thinking you're a snob. You should think about that."

Mary shrugged and walked into the living room to turn on the television and lie down on the brown plaid sofa.

"Peter and Mary don't go together," she thought to herself, thought of shouting into the kitchen to her mother, who stood at the sink snapping green beans. "Unless they're with Paul, unless they're Peter, Paul, and Mary—and he didn't say anything about bringing along someone named Paul."

This made her laugh to herself, turning her face into the crocheted pillow cover her head rested on, the roughness of the yarn scratching her skin. Her glazed eyes stared at a woman in a soap opera on the television screen. She reached for a magazine on the coffee table, then stopped momentarily.

"And Peter denied that he knew Jesus three times the night Jesus died," she wanted to scream into the kitchen. "He was a coward, a wimp. But Mary Magdalene washed his feet with her tears."

At this thought she turned completely onto her stomach, pressing the front of her body hard against the sofa cushions. Soon she drifted off to sleep.

It had been a summer of feeling tired, inexplicably tired, falling into restless sleep early in the evening, even in the middle of the afternoon, on the sofa in front of the TV, or on her bed, listening to records. She wasn't working hard enough to be this tired, she knew (her mother reminded her of this often enough). She helped out some in her mother's garden, and peeled, chopped, and parboiled vegetables and fruits, preparing them for freezing or canning. She babysat for various neighbors, baked cookies for the church Bible School program.

Often on weekends she went swimming at a nearby lake with her friends Pam and Trish. They coated their bodies with suntan oil until the smell of cocoa butter filled the air around them. Mary loved the way the hot afternoon sun felt on her shiny, oiled skin, loved the golden tan that was deepening on her strong legs, liked to watch the play of sunlight on the blond hair on her forearms. She and Pam and Trish laughed and talked about other kids on the makeshift beach (complete with sand imported from somewhere), sneaked occasional cigarettes, their heads held low to the ground as they lay on their bellies, their bikini tops unfastened like those of all the other girls.

But the problem with trips to the lake was that all the same old pressures from school came back again. Pam and Trish were there to look for certain boys, to try to find a reason to talk to them, to do their best to preen in the midst of all their self-consciousness. Why couldn't they just have their *own* beach, Mary often thought to herself. Somewhere they could just laugh and talk and complain about their parents and wonder what it would be like to live someplace else, maybe a city, what their lives might be like there.

It was shaping up to be a rare summer, with good rain, but not too much of it. They had a few ripe tomatoes by the Fourth of July—a good sign. Her father kept busy farming the small piece of land he still owned. Too many summers unlike this atypical one had forced him to sell pieces of his grandfather's farm, bit by bit, to his neighbor. To supplement his income from the farm, he worked a few days a week for the Rural Electric Company, driving through the countryside to read meters and put new identification tags on electric poles.

One evening as Mary lay dozing on the sofa in front of "Wheel of Fortune" after supper, her father brought in his cup of coffee and sat down in his recliner, as always. But this time, instead of gathering together the sections of the morning paper, he turned to Mary and spoke.

"How'd you like to go with me on my Rural Electric rounds tomorrow? You know, ride around out in the country, keep records for me, like you used to do when you were a kid?"

Mary was surprised—strangely flattered, and mildly embarrassed by her father's obvious attempt to wake her up, to get her off the sofa for a day. But she also felt rather hesitant to spend a long day driving through the country with her silent father. When she was younger, it hadn't bothered her, but now his quiet manner unnerved her, made her wonder what he was thinking.

But then she considered the alternatives: watching Bev Turner's three children, all under age four. Or spending the morning in the already-hot kitchen with her mother, cutting stems from tomatoes, cooking them slowly for hours, peering over the huge steaming pots, nearly overwhelmed by the pungent aroma that became heavy and sour after hours of smelling it. Then sliding the hot, wrinkled skin from the pulpy inside, pressing dozens and dozens through a collander with a large, flat wooden spoon, the juice and seeds oozing along her fingers and down her wrists. And finally pouring the juice through a funnel into the old, sterilized Ball jars.

Her mother seemed to revel in the whole process, finding some sort of release in the physicality of it all, after nine long months of attempting to hold the attention of a room full of third graders. But Mary found no joy in it; instead, it seemed to make her feel even more tired than she had before, if that was possible.

"Okay," Mary finally answered. "I think that would be okay."

"Okay," her father said, and he turned to the sports pages.

They left the house at eight o'clock the next morning, driving down the narrow gravel road that led away from their house in her father's old Ford pick-up. It had rained the night before, and the air, though humid, still held the sweet coolness of early morning. A light mist rose from the soybean fields on either side of them, and the damp, green smell reached them through their open windows.

Mary poured them both coffee from her father's big old silver thermos, and they drove for thirty miles or so, over curving country roads, to the next county over. When they reached the area they were to cover that day, Mary's father parked the truck at the side of the road and handed Mary a clipboard and a pencil. She tromped alongside him through the field, following the wires from pole to pole, copying down old and new numbers as her father called them out while nailing up the new metal tags. Eventually they would make their way back to the truck, then drive to the next line that had been marked for retagging.

Later in the morning, they drove down a long lane toward a simple frame farmhouse. Mary saw the wagon outside the old but tidy wooden barn in the back and realized it was an Amish farm. Just then a man in worn overalls, with a long beard and a weathered brown face, rounded the house and walked toward the truck. Mary's father got out of the truck and went to shake the man's hand, and they talked briefly. Soon Mary's father walked up to her window.

"There's just a few poles to get in their front pasture there. Why don't you just stay here and transfer some of those numbers to the other forms while I go back and get 'em."

Mary nodded and handed her father the clipboard. She knew her father was doing this in consideration of the family, and she was glad of it. She felt self-conscious enough under the staring eyes of the two girls in ankle-length cotton dresses (one of them about her age) who had come out onto the front porch. She had no desire to get out of the truck, exposing her gym shorts and bare, tanned legs.

When her father returned, they drove back down the lane and along the road for a short distance, to a shaded glen beside the road with a picnic table, to have their lunch—ham sandwiches, fruit, and two big squares of banana cake, packed for them by Mary's mother that morning. The noon sun was now high and hot, but it was comfortable in the shade.

"It seems kind of strange," Mary said, after they had positioned themselves at the picnic table and spread out their lunch, "for there to be electric lines running over an Amish farm."

Her father chuckled lightly as he bit into his sandwich. "Does, doesn't it? They had a lawsuit over it back when the Rural Electric was first putting in the lines."

"Really? What happened?"

"Well, the Rural Electric won. And now of course most of the Amish have at least some electricity in their homes, you know."

Respectful, even admiring, as he was of the simpler values and lives of the Amish, her father was a firm believer in the progress wrought by the Rural Electric. His father had been one of those most actively involved in bringing electric power to rural Kosciusko County, back in the thirties.

That topic exhausted, Mary could think of nothing else to say, and they went on eating for several minutes in silence. She grew uncomfortable, as she knew she would when facing her father across a picnic table for lunch. Remembering that her father liked to sit on the ground, back against a tree, and linger over a pipe after these lunches (something he seldom did at home), Mary took another quick bite of her sandwich and asked if he'd mind if she explored a bit in the woods.

"Suit yourself," he said. "But keep an eye out for copperheads—they're thick this year."

Relieved, Mary grabbed her piece of cake and headed for the little trail that led from the glen into the surrounding woods. She realized that the prospect of a copperhead snake crossing her path frightened her much less than that of staying at that table to endure more of her father's uncomfortable silence. She couldn't imagine what he was thinking, but she always assumed it was something vaguely critical of her, her lethargy, her aloofness, her general lack of interest in the things he and her mother seemed to care about.

A hundred yards or so into the woods, Mary came upon a clearing, and was amazed to see a small, perfectly clear pond. On the other side of it was a neatly mowed, grassy knoll—a dam, actually; it was a man-made pond.

Who built this? Mary wondered. She walked around the pond toward the dam, staring into the crystal-clear water. She saw an occasional bluegill dart by below shadows of the dragonflies that hovered above the surface. At the water's edge, tall cattails waved in the light breeze.

As she approached the dam, Mary's excitement grew. This could be it! This could be her and Trish and Pam's private beach. Probably some farmer came here in the early morning or at dusk to fish, but in the afternoon there would be no one around. They could spread their towels on the dam, talk and laugh and smoke without having to worry about who was watching, talk about whatever they wanted to talk about without being distracted by boys, or which popular girl had a new suit, or which one was letting her boyfriend sneak furtive feels while he put suntan oil on her back and shoulders. Elated, she climbed the slight incline to the top of the dam.

When she reached the top she dropped suddenly to her knees. Quickly she lay down on her stomach and slid slowly backwards, hiding as best she could while still peering over the top.

Directly below the dam was a soybean field, and not fifty yards from her was a young man in mud-caked trousers, pushing a wooden plow. He'd taken off his white shirt and stuffed it into the back waist of his trousers. He appeared to be about 18 or so, and his arms and back were muscular and tanned.

It dawned on Mary then. This land must be part of the Amish family's farm. She knew she'd never seen this boy before; if he'd gone to one of the local high schools, she would have remembered him.

He was beautiful. His smooth arms curved gracefully and powerfully toward the plow, and his broad back broke into a perfect pattern of muscular lines as he struggled to work the plow through the heavy, wet soil. The field was a large one, of a size that all the farmers she knew would need a tractor to plow. But when he turned to face her, Mary saw that, despite the heavy labor, his face showed no sign of pain or struggle. He looked strangely content, as if loosening the soil, giving these plants room and air to breathe, somehow loosened something in him, too—gave him some kind of freedom.

His sandy hair was bleached almost blond by the sun, and he had a closely trimmed beard. His chest was hairy as well, and as her eyes traced the pattern of the hair, much as she'd followed the electrical wires overhead, down to his tapered waist, Mary held her breath as she felt the familiar tingling begin inside her.

Watching him, she thought suddenly of a birthday party she had gone to when she was twelve. It was for a boy who was two years older than she, the son of the principal at her mother's school, and it was held in the basement rec room of his house in town. Some of the boys at the party had brought in little bottles of whiskey under their sweatshirts, and they were mixing it with the Cokes. Before long, Mary found herself in a dark corner of the rec room with the principal's son. He kissed her, and she was shocked to feel his wet tongue on her teeth, urging them open. He held her at the waist with one hand, and moved the other one up to feel her breast. She stood, terrified, allowing him to explore her mouth with his tongue, her small breast with his fluttering fingers. She felt an odd mixture of sensations, but primarily revulsion; yet she felt powerless to move away from him. Finally he pulled away and they rejoined the party. She sat nervously, waiting for the party to end, relieved when at last her friend Patty's mother arrived to drive them both back home to the country.

The next day, plagued by a vague but nagging guilt, Mary told her mother what had happened. She knew, from Sunday School sessions, that she shouldn't have drunk any of the Coke with whiskey, and from pamphlets her mother had given her, that she should not have let the principal's son touch her breast. But she had been so afraid! She would tell her mother this, tell her all of it; she knew she could find relief only if she confessed what she had done.

When she told her, Mary's mother took her in her arms and said, "Oh, my poor baby," and Mary felt suddenly transported, felt a huge burden lifted from her shoulders. When her mother took her hands, pulling them both to their knees to pray to Jesus for forgiveness, Mary's eyes burned with tears of joy. She had sinned, but she would be forgiven.

Mary thought now about her mother's faith, her abiding concern over her daughter's soul. Mary had stopped confessing everything to her mother, though really there wasn't all that much to confess. But then she thought with burning shame of the ways she had touched herself, alone in her bedroom, the feelings she had given herself, worst of all, the feelings she had when she closed her eyes and pictured Mary Magdalene lovingly stroking Jesus's feet and ankles, caressing them with her long hair.

Mary continued to go to church and Sunday School with her mother and father. She prayed for forgiveness for her sinful thoughts. But try as she might, she couldn't make the insistent tingling go away. It was as if there were something in her that longed to come out, that yearned to pour from her body, like tears and thick oil, like the love of Mary Magdalene.

Even now, watching the young Amish man as his strong arms turned up the rich, dark dirt—one solid motion, arm to plow to earth—she felt it. It ached to come out.

"Joseph!"

She was wakened from her reverie by the sound of a young girl's voice. In the distance she recognized the younger Amish girl she had seen earlier on the porch.

"Joseph! Come in for lunch!"

The young man laid his plow down gently and started walking toward the house, pulling on his long-sleeved white shirt. Mary scrambled down the dam and hurried back to the glen beside the road. She knew her father would wonder what had become of her.

Back in the truck, winding through the countryside again, Mary held her hand out the window, letting her fingers lightly graze the silky yet scratchy leaves in a field of tall corn. She thought again about the principal's son. Through most of high school he'd been a hood, a druggie—hence someone who didn't look twice at her. But then two years ago, during his senior year, he and his girlfriend, a popular girl named Janet, were born again. Along with several other of the richer, more popular high school kids, they had joined a church that seemed to have sprung up overnight (as churches often did in their county) in a neighboring town. Called the New Assembly of God, it featured a reformed alcoholic, ex-bank president preacher who had received the call one night while sipping whiskey and watching the Midnight Meditation on late-night television.

Mary had been invited once, by one of the teenage members, to join them on a retreat at a nearby state park. She planned to go, but then changed her mind at the last minute. One feature of these weekend retreats, she knew, was some kind of personal testimonial before the entire group, and she was terrified of making a spectacle of herself in this way.

Also, she had heard stories of how the more inspired, more deeply spiritual of the young members sometimes spoke in tongues, their bodies convulsed by some outside force, strange mutterings and gurglings pouring from their throats, rolling rapidly off their tongues, leaving them, at last, spent but deeply at peace. This frightened Mary more than the testimonials, and in a far different way. She was intrigued, but also afraid.

When she and her father got home that evening, Mary called Pam. "You have to see this pond—you won't believe it! And there's this grassy dam that will be perfect for laying out . . ."

When Pam started to protest that she didn't want to miss out on the action at the lake, Mary played her trump card.

"But wait, there's more. There's this gorgeous Amish guy, about eighteen or so, who works in this field right below the dam. Shirtless, no less—pretty daring for an Amish guy, right? And you won't even believe his body—perfect tan, incredible muscles."

It worked, as she'd known it would. They made plans to go the next day. Pam would call Trish, who could probably get her mother's car for the afternoon.

But after she hung up, Mary felt a vague uneasiness, almost a sort of guilt, over going on so about Joseph. She told herself that it was only to get Pam and Trish to go there with her, so they could have their own private beach like she'd always wanted. And yet she couldn't help feeling that she had wronged him, this young man she didn't even know, in some way. But she shook it off, deciding that he'd never even know, and what he didn't know couldn't hurt him.

The next morning Mary iced down diet sodas in a cooler and popped a bag full of popcorn to take along. She chose a pair of red nylon running shorts that accentuated her long legs and matched her bandeau-style bikini top for the occasion. She was waiting on the back steps when Trish drove down the gravel lane, honking loudly.

When they got to the pond and climbed to the top of the dam, Joseph was nowhere in sight.

Trish cocked an eyebrow at Mary, and Mary noticed she was wearing a thin line of eyeliner. "So where is this Greek god, Mare? You didn't make him up just to get us out here, did you?"

"He'll be here, don't worry. He's probably just in for lunch right now."

Mary spread her beach towel on the grassy incline, letting it slope toward the pond so she would be able to hide herself if and when Joseph did show up, and started arranging her suntan oil, water bottle, soda container, and the like. The other girls did the same.

Soon they were on their backs, laughing at a joke Trish told them, and Mary felt herself start to relax, start to believe that everything would be all right and they would have a good time. She rolled over onto her stomach and glanced toward the field just in time to see Joseph approaching.

Immediately she shushed Pam and Trish and signaled them to look in his direction with a tilt of her head. They scrambled onto their stomachs, and all three stayed low to the ground, their heads peering over the top of the dam.

Joseph slowly and methodically unbuttoned his shirt and once again tucked it into the back of his trousers. He picked up the plow and started moving down a row of the field, his back to them.

Pam and Trish murmured appreciatively and whispered excitedly. Soon their whispers turned to giggles, and Mary tried in vain to quiet them. She watched, with growing panic, as Joseph reached the end of a row and turned to come back in their direction. Suddenly, before Mary could stop them, Pam and Trish were sitting up, preening, as if by instinct, just as they did at the lake—hands flying to smooth hair, adjust bathing suit tops, wipe tiny lines of sweat from the tops of their lips.

It had become a nightmare, a horrible mistake, and Mary seemed to see it all in slow motion. Joseph heard the girls giggling and looked up to see them there. He blushed crimson, an expression of pained confusion passing over his face. He dropped the plow suddenly in the middle of the field and hurried away, back toward the house.

Pam and Trish held their mouths, desperately trying to restrain their laughter, and glanced nervously at Mary. She had already pulled on her shorts and begun gathering her things.

"Come on." She spat the words at them in her fury. "Let's get out of here."

They rode home in silence.

For the next three days, it rained—the steady showers and low, rumbling skies of a summer storm. Mary wandered around the house nervously, her strange listlessness suddenly replaced by a stranger restlessness. Her mother looked at her with a puzzled expression as she offered to shell peas, shuck corn—anything to occupy her hands, if not her mind. At night, instead of sleeping heavily like before, she tossed and turned, constantly replaying the scene at the dam in her mind, struggling to think of a way to make it up to Joseph, to give him back the peace he had had as he plowed, before the day he looked up to see three giggling teenage girls watching him.

One evening early the next week, she asked her father where he would be going to tag poles that week.

"Well, same general area we were in last week, I reckon. Still some more to do there."

"Could I come with you again? And do you think we could have lunch at the same place? I'd like to go back to that pond again."

Her father grinned at her, obviously pleased and a little surprised. "Well, sure, if you want to." And as an afterthought, "What'd you find back there, a boy swimming in that pond or something?"

This time when they drove down the lane at eight o'clock in the morning, the sky was cloudy and gray, though the rain had stopped for a time. Big raindrops would fall from the low-hanging branches of trees, splattering on the windshield, as they drove through wooded areas.

Her father seemed a bit more talkative than usual, and Mary took the opportunity to ask him what he thought of Amish farming practices.

"I mean, doesn't it seem kind of ridiculous to you for them to limit themselves like that, to use clunky old wooden plows when they own all that land and could make so much more use of it if they just got some real machinery?" (This was the theory of wasted space and potential, one she'd heard argued many times by younger farmers, and by the boys she knew in school who also lived on farms. As a girl, it hadn't really occurred to her to have an opinion on this. Until now.)

"Well, you know they approach their land in a very different way. I guess you could say they respect it more. And it has to do with their faith, too. They believe you should just keep your needs simple, keep your whole life simple. Just kind of let things be, let 'em breathe.

"You know, my dad kind of thought that way. And his dad, too. They believed in progress and all, but they didn't think you should just keep taking in more and more land, more and more live-stock—till you finally have more than you can handle."

He laughed wryly. "Of course, you could argue that that's why I'm out here driving this truck with my clipboard and tags right now, and why our farm is half the size it was at one time."

He grinned at her sheepishly, and she smiled at him, touched by this honesty and, for once, not at all embarrassed.

They stopped for lunch at the glen beside the road, as planned, but they ate inside the truck because it had started to drizzle a bit. When it seemed to have stopped, Mary said she still wanted to head back to the pond. As she made her way to the path, her father spread his rain poncho on the ground and lit his pipe.

She didn't really expect Joseph to be in the field, but, buoyed by her father's words, feeling strangely strengthened by them, she thought that if he were, perhaps she would apologize to him.

She spread her own slicker on the crest of the dam and lay on her stomach atop it, peering over. He was there again, shirt on this time, struggling even more intently to maneuver the stubborn plow through the sodden soil. It seemed that nothing could keep him away. Watching him, she imagined that he glanced nervously around him, expecting at any minute to hear giggling and whispers.

As she rehearsed in her mind what she might say to him, the damp ground made Mary shiver momentarily, and she found her-self thinking, again, of Mary Magdalene and Jesus. Of her tears and flowing love for him, of his gentle empathy and nonjudgmental love for her, for all around him. The image of Mary Magdalene's damp hair cleansing Jesus's soiled feet, Joseph turning up the near-mud in front of her, her own shivering skin on the wet grass—all these things made Mary want to weep with unspeakable longing. To let the endless tears, and all the unnameable things she felt churning inside her, come pouring, gushing out.

She remembered the time, a year before, when she had stayed home with a headache while her parents went to church on Sunday morning. One of her friends who had gone on one of the First Assembly of God retreats had just described to her how the Holy Spirit had come into the principal's son, and he had spoken in tongues. Pulled to the ground by the force of it, he had closed his eyes and held his arms up to heaven, and suddenly, words in a language no one understood had poured from his lips in a raspy, broken voice. It lasted about a minute, and when it was over, he collapsed onto the ground and his girlfriend Janet hugged him and they cried together.

Walking around the house that Sunday morning, Mary felt something surging inside of her, something she couldn't identify. Her mother had been angry with her for not going to church with them. Her mother was critical of so many things, she thought. Even the kids who went to First Assembly, because they spoke in tongues, which was something she didn't trust.

Stopping in front of the living room picture window that looked out onto the wide field in front of their house, Mary dropped down to her knees. She held her hands out to God, palms open, closed her eyes, and prayed. She poured her heart out to God, and tears flowed down her cheeks.

"Please, God, if it's your will, let your spirit come into me. Let me feel what that's like, let whatever this is that's trapped inside me come out, let me feel whatever it is the others feel."

And she opened her mouth wide, breathing deeply, trying to give whatever it was room to come out, waiting expectantly for it to begin.

But nothing happened. No strange languages. No gurgling or rasping voice. No wave of spiritual bliss.

Mary stayed on her knees on the floor for what seemed like hours, but was actually only about fifteen minutes. When she heard her parents' car on the lane, she hurried up to her room and got back in bed.

* * *

Twisting onto her side and trying to wrap her slicker around her chilled arms as she lay on the dam, Mary pictured the principal's son with his eyes closed, arms reaching up to heaven, strange words coming from his lips, his tongue a vehicle for the Holy Spirit. She remembered his birthday party, when he was fourteen and she was twelve. To this very day, there were times when she could still taste the whiskey on his breath and tongue.

She stared at Joseph and his simple plow. She realized, gradually but certainly, that she would never apologize to him. It occurred to her now that her dry, parched mouth would not even be able to utter his holy name.

A Thief in the Night

About days and times, my friends, we need not write to you, for you know perfectly well that the Day of the Lord comes like a thief in the night. While they are talking of peace and security, all at once calamity is upon them, sudden as the pangs that come upon a woman with child; and there will be no escape.
—1 Thessalonians 5:1-3

There's no reason to sleep curled up and bent. It's not comfortable, it's not good for you and it doesn't protect you from danger. If you're worried about an attack you should stay awake or sleep lightly with limbs unfurled for action.
—Jenny Holzer, from *The Living Series*, 1981–82

They're cutting back service on the Chicago and South Shore railroad again. Fewer and fewer people are riding the electric trains that run between Chicago and South Bend, stopping at various points along the south shore of Lake Michigan. Which means cuts in the budget, fewer trains, and more problems with the ones that are still running. Soon, to get from Michigan City to Chicago, you'll have to have a car. Soon, if you want to get out of Michigan City for some reason, that will be the only way to go.

★ ★ ★

In the morning as she was blowing her hair dry, Lucy gradually became aware of a sustained but distant humming below the whir of air about her ears. She became convinced, immediately, that it was the blare of a warning siren. "It's happened," she thought. "We're at war. They're shooting each other right now, people are running through fields and stepping on land mines, they're spraying chemicals over each other's bodies . . . the desert air is thick with poison and everyone is choking."

She thought of Joey's family the Sunday before, his mother and his sister Jane clicking their tongues over the pictures in the paper, his old Aunt Stella crossing herself somberly, his Uncle Roy hiking his ill-fitting trousers over his fat belly, spouting about tanks and war ("Goddamn Arabs—oughta just blow 'em all away"), his young nephews chasing each other through the living room with toy Ouzis. Through the haze of noise and activity all around him, Joey sat mute in his father's easy chair, the way he always did at his parents' house, staring at the television, sucking down a Budweiser. Lucy stared at him intently for a minute, then realized he was a million miles away. If he'd noticed her staring, he would have given her some gesture of complicity—a wink, a subtle shrug of his broad shoulders—then gone back to the TV. Seeing that he would offer no solace, Lucy went out the back door and walked through the pasture behind his parents' house until Joey was ready to go.

She'd been with him for three months now, and some parts of her presence in this tiny northern Indiana town were more inexplicable than others.

At the beginning of the summer she'd quit her job and moved back from Ann Arbor to South Bend, where her father was a professor at the University of Notre Dame. Her mother had died the winter before, and her brother, who lived in California, had suggested Lucy leave her job and spend the summer with their father in South Bend. Quitting her job meant nothing in particular—everyone knew it was just an interim sort of thing. "Good to take a little time off before graduate school," her father had said, "it'll give you more balance."

Plus this meant being a little closer to her boyfriend Paul, a graduate student at the University of Chicago. She could take the Chicago and South Shore line to see him on weekends, when he'd have a little time to break from his research now and then.

But Lucy hadn't spent a weekend with Paul since July, three months before. The last morning of that last stay, when she announced to Paul that she'd decided to leave early, he'd said, "You knew it would be like this, Lucy. If you can't handle my work demands, you probably *should* just go."

As she finished packing her bag that morning, she'd heard the click of the stereo switch behind her, a few scattered pops of the needle, and the rubbing noise of the turntable as it made several muffled turns. She held her breath, awaiting the sudden surge of violins, the clash of cymbals. Though she knew it was coming any minute, still she jumped, startled, when the music began. This was Paul's sign that his day was underway, and he was not to be disturbed. As she walked out the door, she heard him turn on the shower. The violins trailed her down the hall to the elevator, and she ran from them.

She raced to make the 10:15 train to South Bend. A little over an hour into the journey she was staring out the window at the dingy houses next to the tracks when the train lurched to a sudden halt just outside the Michigan City station. She had just detected a burning, hot-metal smell that seemed to lodge itself in her throat when the conductor announced engine trouble and told the passengers they'd have to leave the train.

It was a steaming hot summer day, with temperatures in the nineties and humidity that turned the air into an unwanted blanket on her shoulders and forearms. Lucy tried waiting inside the station but the lone air conditioner was broken, and no air stirred at the open windows. She went back out to the platform and walked to the very end, where a few spindly branches of an old, overgrown maple arched over the tracks, providing scattered dots of shade.

Joey was part of the crew who were called in to make the repairs, which turned out to be tediously slow. He had seen her there, wilting in the heat, and invited her to wait at his house, near the station.

Now it was September, and after sundown most evenings there was a crispness in the air of this northern Indiana town, a chill that blew off the lake, and except for a few trips home to visit her father, who had immersed himself in his work and seemed, as far as she could tell, to be doing fine, Lucy had not left Joey's house in Michigan City. She had made one phone call to Paul, to tell him she would not be back the next weekend or the next, so he could do his work in peace. And she had a new job, as a receptionist in a medical clinic in downtown Michigan City.

It was this job that she was getting ready for as she dried her hair and listened to the steady whine of what she fully believed to be an announcement of war. She suddenly remembered a time in college when she had gone with Paul and a group of his friends—all two years ahead of her—to a bar they frequented, a rowdy place on the edge of Ann Arbor with country music on the jukebox, crowded with locals. It was a still night, damp from an earlier rain, and the air was warm and heavy.

As she climbed out of the car in the parking lot in front of the bar, she heard a hissing, humming noise overhead and looked up into the electrified air, lit by two faint streetlights and the blinking neon of the sign on the bar. The hair on her arms stood on end. It was radiation, she decided. There had been some kind of explosion, maybe some kind of attack, and they were all standing there in the parking lot being radiated.

She clutched Paul's arm in a panic. "Do you hear that? What's making that noise?"

But Paul laughed at her, reaching his arm around her and pulling her close.

"Lucy, it's just the humming of the telephone wires. They always hum like that—you have to have heard them before." He hurried her forward to catch up with the others.

"Silly kid—did you think it was aliens from outer space or something?"

She let herself be pulled into the bar, but later, when Paul and his friends were on their third pitcher of beer and in the throes of a heated discussion of campus politics, she crept back outside and stared up at the streetlights and the telephone wires. The humming sounded deafeningly loud to her, and she crawled back into the car, pulling herself into a snug, tiny ball in the back seat, where she fell asleep.

Now Lucy was convinced that when she turned off the hair dryer, the low blaring of the siren would still be there. And in fact it was. But instead of a siren warning of war, it was a Chicago and South Shore train, stalled again for some reason on the track that ran behind Joey's house.

* * *

A few blocks away, Clarice Johnson did not even notice the stalled train, though the tracks ran directly behind her kitchen, where she sat heavily on a torn yellow vinyl kitchen chair. Her hands rested absently on the sticky surface of the table, next to puddles of milk at the sides of half-eaten bowls of cereal. The bowls had been abandoned there minutes before by her two grandchildren, when Clarice finally chased them out the door to school. On the wall above her head, in the center of a picture framed in gold, the figure of Christ stood knocking at a closed door. At his feet, in gold lettering, were the words, "He comes like a thief in the night."

Clarice failed to hear the stalled train, humming loudly not fifty yards outside her kitchen window, first because of the blaring television in the next room. Then her son Anthony entered the front door of the house and snapped the TV off angrily, and the next thing she knew he was standing in the kitchen doorway, facing her defiantly, strong arms folded over the wrinkled shirt of his correction officer's uniform. His words blew into her like a furious blast of wind.

"I *gotta* get out of here. I know Michigan City was supposed to be the promised land for you and Daddy, but you know as well as I do it hasn't turned out that way. There's nothing for me here, no chance of getting anywhere out at that goddamn State Pen. I gotta get out of here while I still *can*." He turned abruptly and headed into his room, slamming the door behind him.

Clarice was already running late for her own job at the State Penitentiary, where she worked in the kitchen from ten to six five days a week, before going to her second job, cleaning a doctors' office downtown. But she stopped in the middle of cracking eggs for her son's breakfast, which she prepared each morning before she left, putting it on the table for him just as he got in from working the night shift as a guard. She sat down at the table and tried to steady herself before leaving for the next round of her long day.

When at last she roused herself and called to Anthony that his eggs were ready, she strained to hear his mumbled reply from his room. Only then did she notice the steady whine of the broken-down train.

* * *

"What do you know about this fellow?" her father had asked when Lucy called to tell him she would be staying in Michigan City for a while.

"Not a lot, really," she'd had to admit. Though the one thing she did know, the really crucial thing, was that he was completely trustworthy. Though he was often silent—not exactly withdrawn, but clearly in a different place, removed from her—Lucy knew from the moment she met Joey Christianson that he was utterly, piercingly honest. His watery blue eyes held absolutely no hint of anything but the truth.

When she first saw him, he was gulping water from a sweating bottle in the noon heat of July outside the train station. He wore an old gray T-shirt that was stained with sweat—under the arms, at the small of the back, tracing a path along his breastbone to a narrow point just above the fly of his faded blue jeans—and, Lucy realized, she could smell him, and it was a deep, musky smell that she wanted to keep breathing in. She watched him unblinkingly, as if unaware that he could see her as well, and it took a moment for her to remember to exhale.

He was thin but solidly built, his hair was dark and curly but trimmed close, and it occurred to Lucy that he reminded her, unmistakably, of an animal in a zoo—not a caged one but one in a broader space, with pools and trees and rocks for climbing and sunning, held in by a simple fence. As she stared at him, she felt something start up inside her, first a funny clicking in her chest, then what felt like the flutter of a crazily wagging tail inside her stomach.

He felt her staring at him then, and turned to look back. It was then that he approached her where she stood, hot and at a loss, at the end of the platform, her overstuffed knapsack leaning awkwardly at her ankles like a burdensome child.

"Looks like we'll be workin' on this for a while," he said to her. "You need a place to wait?"

What did she know about Joey Christianson? She knew he was thirty-four years old, and his last name was an Anglicization of his grandfather's surname, Cristiani. That that grandfather had been an Italian immigrant who worked on the railroads in the early part of the century and lived until he died in the house that Joey lived in now. The house was in a neighborhood now occupied mostly by blacks and poor whites, whose compact frame houses now faced or stood in front of the Chicago and South Shore railroad tracks.

Occasionally, at the neighborhood grocery store, Lucy would run into Clarice Johnson, the woman who cleaned the doctors' office where she worked. The first time it happened the two women discovered that they lived only a few blocks apart. Lucy thought she noticed a look of surprise on Clarice's face, a curiously raised eyebrow, and she felt suddenly compelled to explain her presence in the neighborhood.

"I'm not actually from Michigan City," she began breathlessly. "I mean, not originally. You see, my father lives in South Bend and I was taking the train back and forth from Chicago, and well anyway, to make a long story short I met a man who lives here—he lives in his grandfather's old house, actually—his grandfather used to work on the railroad—and well, anyway, I'm living with him right now."

She laughed nervously. "I'm not sure what all that has to do with anything, really!" she said at last. And she stared helplessly at Clarice, flushed and embarrassed and not sure what to do next. Clarice, who had listened attentively, simply nodded. Then she touched Lucy's arm and said softly, "There's no need to explain what you're doin' here. And if you've found a good man here in Michigan City, don't be in any hurry to get back on that train to Chicago. Already plenty of folks there. Just plant your feet and thank God for what he's given you, Lucy. You remember that."

Their paths seldom crossed at the office, as Clarice generally arrived after Lucy had already left for the day. On the few occasions when Lucy stayed late for some reason, Clarice would race back to clean one of the examining rooms in the back after a hurried hello, and Lucy never mustered the nerve to ask her more about the advice she'd given her that day. "Plant your feet." How could she know that was the right thing to do?

Joey earned enough money from the periodic construction work he did to move out of his grandfather's house, to get a nice new apartment in a complex with a swimming pool or a lake, even a small house in the subdivision at the outskirts of Michigan City, where his parents lived. His relatives were always urging him to move out. "I can't see why you want to stay on there," his mother had whined during lunch the Sunday before, and reaching for the plate of pot roast, his sister piped in with, "If it was *me* I'd be afraid to be alone at night in a neighborhood like that."

"It's true you should think about Lucy," Joey's father added in his most deepset, serious voice. He cleared his throat and added, "That is, if the two of you are planning on staying together . . ."

"I don't want Joey to move on my account," Lucy had responded, barely audibly, looking to Joey for support. But as always, Joey chose to remain silent in the face of his family's questions, acting as if he hadn't heard a word that was said, finishing his meal and then excusing himself to go back to the football game on TV. Everyone else acted as if nothing had been said as well, immediately turning back to their food and a discussion of two neighbors who were getting a divorce.

And Lucy excused herself and went outside, aware that the women in Joey's family would be clicking their tongues once again, this time over the fact that she wasn't bothering to help with the dishes.

Despite his family's protests, Joey stayed in his grandfather's house, where he worked to keep the lawn neat, the porch and roof in good repair, the outside painted a clean white, and the inside tidy and simple, furnished much as it had been when his grandparents were alive. This was one of several things about Joey Christianson that made him a Michigan City anomaly.

Another was the fact that at age thirty-four he had never been married, and though he occasionally had a girlfriend, he rarely stayed with anyone for long. He didn't care much for frequenting the bars with his friends from the construction crews, and when they sat around someone's living room, drinking beer and watching porn videos, he was known to station himself in a distant corner and pull out a magazine.

He was a skilled carpenter, and that first afternoon as she waited for the train to be repaired, Lucy wandered through the small rooms of his neat little house in awe, stumbling upon a beautiful cherry table, a gleaming walnut pie safe, and, in the hallway outside his bedroom, a full-size oak grandfather clock. When he returned at one point to check on her and she asked him where he'd gotten such gorgeous furniture, he seemed genuinely embarrassed to tell her he had made it all.

He was an oddly gentle lover—the gentleness seeming to her an unusual accompaniment to his animal-like strength and silence. She made love to him the evening of the first day she met him, instead of taking the train, repaired at last at about five o'clock, on to South Bend. She realized, after the second time they made love that night, that he would not fall asleep. But he also would not leave her side. He lay there watching her, softly stroking her arm or her hair, but always intently watching her face, as if he were afraid that if he looked away, she would suddenly be gone.

At one point his staring began to make her nervous, and she looked back into his eyes and smiled uncomfortably. He smiled back and shook his head slowly. "They never get it right in the movies," he said.

"What do you mean?" she asked, surprised to hear him speaking after so long a silence.

"I mean when the guys get those porn movies, I just can't watch them because it always looks like a couple of squealing pigs, or like two people sweating and grunting over something between them they can't move."

She laughed and nodded. "But how about other movies, you know, regular ones, not porn ones," she asked. "Do you think they ever get it right in those love scenes?"

"Well, no, because in Hollywood love scenes, the bodies always look too perfect, you know, too clean and perfectly dry, like if you reached out to touch one it'd be cold as ice. Or else they don't even look like real bodies at all—just a couple fuzzy outlines in the dark, maybe just a hand climbing over what *might* be a backside, maybe."

"So how do you think they could get it right?"

"Well, they shouldn't leave out the sweat," he said, pausing to lick the damp, curling red hair at the nape of her neck, the freckles on her sticky chest and shoulders. "And they should just show a person's body like it is," and he paused to smooth his hand along the length of her thin, pale side. "But just because there's sweat it doesn't have to look like it's such hard work. It should just look like what it is."

"Which is what, exactly?" she asked teasingly.

He sighed then and said, "I don't know, I'm tired of words," and then he pulled her on top of him.

It was, she realized later, one of the longer conversations they'd had. And, at that point, she had felt charmed by the fact that Joey was a man who rather quickly grew tired of words.

* * *

Later that day, as she went about her business in the kitchen of the State Penitentiary, Clarice felt restless and frustrated by the monotony of the work in a way that was unusual for her. At the same time, though, she felt bone-weary, exhausted by the effort of lifting her body onto a footstool to reach the rows of industrial-sized cans of pork and beans. She was a large woman, and the physically demanding work in the kitchen often left her breathing hard, pausing to rest on a worn metal folding chair in the corner.

Usually, she did her best to rest with a smile on her face, praying in a whisper, thanking Jesus for this work, for a house of her own, money to feed her grandchildren, and a son who was doing his best to follow in his father's footsteps.

She and Leon married when he was eighteen and she was seventeen, then immediately boarded a Chicago and South Shore train for Michigan City, dying to escape their families' crowded apartments on the south side of Chicago. They had known each other since they were children in Mississippi. In 1960, Leon's brother wrote to tell him there were jobs for both of them for the asking at the State Penitentiary, that before long they'd have enough set aside to buy one of the little houses along the railroad tracks. They left two weeks after the letter arrived.

Those were years of such unbelievable hope that it shocked, almost embarrassed her even, to think of it now. As she stood and began cutting big slabs of cheese into uniform rectangles, Clarice remembered watching Dr. King on television while her babies slept, snug and secure in the next room, and her husband worked the night shift. When he arrived home in the morning, she would put his breakfast on the table and hurry out the door to get the bus out to her job in the kitchen, singing gaily as she walked to the corner. And on Sundays, the day they both had off, they'd dress the children in their finest clothes and go off together to services at the First Baptist Church—the church she and Leon had helped found, in the old Elks Lodge next to the train station.

After church, she would go home with the baby, and Leon would take Anthony to the corner store to buy him penny candy and talk to him about his dreams. When they got back, Leon would reach his strong arms around her where she stood at the stove, so much thinner and happier then, and he would say, "That boy's gonna make something of himself, Clarice, you watch. And he'll have a whole new world to do it in. Mark my words, nothin's gonna get in his way."

She loved the way he said her name, drawing out the second syllable that way: "Clar-eeeece." Her father had always pronounced her name like "Clarence," wishing, she knew, that she had been a boy.

Life at home with her father had not been easy, but from the time she was a small child, Leon had been there to make her laugh. She still remembered the day when she was fourteen, when she looked at Leon and suddenly saw, for the first time, not a laughing, clowning boy, but a smooth-skinned young man with lines of muscle pushing out from under his shirt sleeves. What had happened, she wondered, had he changed overnight?

And where had those huge, black-pool eyes come from? She'd never really looked at his eyes, she realized, since they were usually crinkled up or closed completely with laughter. But suddenly there they were, and they were black as night, and she did not quite know what to make of it when, gazing into them, she felt a nighttime chill down her spine as he took her hand one evening and said, "Come on, Clarice. Walk down to the creek with me."

Thinking back on that moment she didn't know whether to laugh at her childish bewilderment or cry over the deep pain in her chest every time she thought, now, of Leon's beautiful, black-pool eyes. All the time she knew him, those eyes never failed to give her that same nighttime chill, to make her shudder with loving him.

Anthony had loved Leon deeply, too. And he had wanted to make his father proud, she knew. But the new world Leon looked forward to in 1965 never happened somehow, and in 1968 Dr. King was dead, and so was Leon.

When she reminds Anthony of his father's dream for him, he stares at her like she's a total stranger, lost in a world of fantasy. She's tried reminding him of what Chicago has done for his sister, who can't even care for her own children, but to no avail. Nor has it helped to remind him of how his father died. Leon had taken the train over to Chicago to visit his ailing mother. Walking back from the hospital to his cousin's apartment one night he was mugged, stabbed five times, and left in a pool of blood on the sidewalk.

In Clarice Johnson's experience, nothing good has ever come of taking the South Shore line over to Chicago.

* * *

Across town, at the clinic, Lucy stared out from behind the receptionist's desk at a nearly deserted waiting room. It was three o'clock, and she'd finished all the bookkeeping and filing and put aside her novel; she was thinking again about war, about last Sunday's visit to Joey's parents' house. When he finally came to tell her it was time to go that afternoon, she found that she could not muster the energy to go back into the house to tell his relatives goodbye. She couldn't, she realized, say thank you to them with the slightest shred of honesty. She couldn't feel that there was anything at all to thank them for.

It didn't matter to Joey. He didn't expect her to say anything at all to his parents. Sunday afternoon visits there were simply part of the carefully orchestrated ritual of his life, a ritual that allowed for a certain amount of contact with family and friends, but set definite limits on how far that contact would go. He seemed happiest, she thought, when he was working with wood. She watched him sometimes in his basement workshop, and the way he handled the smooth pieces—so delicately, almost lovingly, like a violinist carefully fingering strings and bow—made her ache sometimes with sadness and longing, for what she wasn't sure.

Once she suggested to him that he could probably make a lot of money if he tried to sell some of his pieces somewhere like Ann Arbor or Chicago. "I've seen things at the craft shows in Ann Arbor that weren't half as good as yours—and they sell for thousands of dollars," she said.

She had meant to flatter him, but when she said this he turned sullen. "I don't make these to sell, Lucy," he said, lifting a large oak plank onto his workbench. Before he began to sand its edges he looked over at her and said, "Maybe you're just trying to put me where *you'd* like to be."

It was true that Joey's plan for his life was one she couldn't quite grasp, just as she so often felt she could not reach him. Though his loving her could feel like the tenderest, closest thing she had ever known, she sometimes felt separated from him by a vast and empty desert when she was sitting right beside him.

He did ask her questions. On the drive home from his parents' house that Sunday, he asked, "What did you do on Sundays when you were growing up? Did you go to church?"

"Sometimes, but not that often," she answered. "What I remember about Sundays were the faculty wife afternoon teas." She shook her head and laughed wryly at the memory, covering her eyes.

Joey smiled over at her, hoping to be let in on the joke. "What were those?"

"Well, they were these little gatherings for professors' wives.

They weren't really anything official. It was just this group of women who got all dressed up and had tea and little cookies and so forth and gossiped for a couple hours at someone's house."

"And you went along with your mother?"

"Yeah, and I was usually the only kid there because most of these women were quite a bit older than my mother and, you know, their children weren't around any more.

"I have this very distinct memory of being at the dean's house—the dean's wife was always really involved in these things. My dad used to say that was how the dean got all the dirt on the faculty. I remember sitting on the stairs, on this incredibly soft, dusty blue carpet, playing with my doll. When I looked to my right, all I could see was a row of ladies' legs in nylon stockings, all primly crossed at the ankle. When I looked to my left, all I could see was all these coats with fur collars hanging on a coat rack. One of them had a whole animal around the collar, head and all—remember those coats? I don't know what it was, but its beady little eyes were staring right at me." She laughed softly again, shaking her head.

"Were you scared?"

"Terrified! I ran out to sit on my mother's lap. She held me there, but you can believe she continued to sit very properly. God, I can still smell those women's perfumes all mixed together—and mixed with cigarette smoke, too. Lots of people still smoked then, even the faculty wives."

"Why'd your mother go if they were all so much older?"

"I don't know. I guess she thought it was expected of her or something." Lucy sighed and stared out the window at the tumble-down houses lining the street that led to Joey's house.

"Actually, I think my mother was pretty bored by the whole thing. I guess maybe she was just that lonely." Lucy shifted in her seat and adjusted the sun visor in front of her. "I'm not really sure."

Joey pulled into the driveway and turned off the engine, then turned to face her. She wanted to cry suddenly, though she wasn't sure why.

"You know, when you were standing out there, out in the back yard at Mom and Dad's, you reminded me of the teacher I had in sixth grade."

Lucy raised an eyebrow and looked at him, not quite seeing the connection.

"She was young and kind of pretty, though you wouldn't really know it. She had long blonde hair that she always wore back in a braid, and she wore big baggy skirts and long blouses. Her name was Mercy Bryson."

Lucy smiled. "You're kidding."

"No, I'm serious. We called her Miss Mercy. Everyone thought she was a little strange, with a name like that and the way she dressed and so forth. Plus she didn't have a car; she always walked or rode a bike around town. She kept pretty much to herself, I think. I always felt kind of sorry for her.

"She was a good teacher, and I think everyone kind of liked her but they wouldn't admit it. One day I rode my bike down to the drugstore with a couple friends. We were standing at the comic book rack, which was right by the door, drinking our Cokes and reading comics. I looked up and saw Miss Mercy come out of the bank across the street. She was crying, and I went and stood at the door and watched her. She just walked up Main Street real slow, kind of weaving, like she wasn't watching where she was going. I kept on watching her till she went over the top of the hill and I couldn't see her anymore. I guess I kind of wanted to do something for her, I don't know."

"Poor Miss Mercy," Lucy said, only half joking. "I wonder what happened at the bank."

"I never found out. She left after the end of that year. Somebody said she moved to Chicago." He paused. "I always wondered what happened to her."

Lucy felt overwhelmingly sad, suddenly. Without really thinking, she said, "I wonder what she was doing in Michigan City in the first place."

When she saw the look on Joey's face, the sudden, palpable distance in his eyes, she immediately regretted her words.

"I wouldn't know," he said, and he opened the car door and got out. When she came inside a minute later, the TV was on and Joey was seated in front of it with a book. She paused but he didn't look up, and she went upstairs to bed.

She was rooting around for what it was she had wanted to say to Joey at that moment, struggling to form the words in her mind, when one of the doctors came to tell her he was leaving. It was four o'clock. She stretched and yawned, amazed at how exhausted she felt after such an uneventful day. She stared at the phone, thinking, as she had been for some time now, about calling Paul. She picked up the receiver, then realized she'd forgotten his number. She pulled her address book out of her bag, but as she did, she remembered that Sunday morning in July, remembered holding her breath as she zipped her bag, hearing the menacing, muted spinning of the turntable, waiting for the inevitable rush of violins.

And suddenly she recalled being ten years old, new to their house and neighborhood in South Bend, walking quietly into her father's study in search of her mother. When she reached the door she stopped, shocked to see her mother in tears, digging her nails into her palms as she stood facing Lucy's father, repeating over and over—in a near whisper, as if to herself—"I can't take it, David. I just can't take it anymore." Lucy stood there in the door, unable to move, watching as her father handed her mother his handkerchief, turning his back to her and returning to his desk as he said, "Please Ellen, try to calm down. I have so much work to do."

Her mother cried even harder, but still—incredibly—silently, now covering her mouth with her hand. She turned toward the door just in time to catch a glimpse of her daughter, who ran from the sight, ashamed, somehow embarrassed for her mother, appalled at what she had seen. A record was turning on her father's wobbly old turntable—"Serenade for Strings," his favorite—and the high notes of the violins followed Lucy as she ran. She covered her ears with her hands and hurried out the front door, jumping onto her bicycle and riding as fast as she could down the block. But still she heard the screeching of the violins, whining, screaming in her ears. She rode and rode, furiously, until her own panting and the pounding of blood in her ears finally drowned the insistent sound of the strings.

Lucy put the address book down on her desk, next to the phone. Instead of dialing she reached for her novel, forcing herself to concentrate, shutting out everything else. She read for an hour, until it was time to go home.

* * *

Clarice shoved the last rack of sticky plastic trays into the dishwasher with a grunt, turned on the machine, and reached around to untie her apron. Her arms ached and her feet were tired. She reached for her jacket on its hook in the back room, methodically replacing it with the apron, got her bag from her locker, and hurried to the parking lot. Forty-five minutes to get home, get something heated up for the children's supper, then get downtown to the doctors' office.

As she drove she prayed that Anthony would still be there, asleep in his room in preparation for going back to work tonight. Maybe if she could get him to church with her on Sunday, she thought, he'd forget about this nonsense of going to Chicago. "Just keep him off that train for a while longer," she prayed. "Please, Lord."

* * *

Instead of going right home that evening, Lucy stopped for a drink downtown. As she sat in a corner sipping a beer and watching the crowd at the bar, she kept picturing Miss Mercy, walking aimlessly up Main Street until she reached the top of the hill and disappeared. And there in the door of the drugstore she saw Joey, standing and staring in his gray T-shirt and jeans, looking the way he'd looked the day she met him. His eyes were full of feeling, but his mouth stayed closed, his arms folded in front of him.

She spotted a pay phone in the hall behind her, and reached into her bag for her address book. Then she remembered that she'd left it at the clinic. She left three dollars on the table and headed back.

* * *

At 6:35 PM Clarice is halfway done cleaning the reception area and waiting room when she stops for a moment, realizing she feels dizzy and weak. She hasn't eaten anything since morning she suddenly remembers. Exhausted, she collapses onto a sofa in the waiting room. She takes off her glasses and leans back in the darkening room, rubbing her eyes.

Just then the door opens and Lucy walks in. When she sees Clarice she jumps, startled, then realizes who she is and begins to stumble through an apology.

"Oh, I'm sorry, Clarice—I hope I didn't scare you. I didn't expect you to be out here in front. I just, I forgot my address book, and I needed it just now, and I was still downtown having a quick drink so—"

She stops talking suddenly, realizing she is saying too much, so much more than is necessary. Then she notices Clarice's eyes. She's never seen her without her glasses.

"Are you okay, Clarice?"

"Yes, yes, honey, I'm fine. Don't get worried now—and don't tell the doctors you found me nappin' on the job!"

Clarice laughs nervously and now she's all apologies, and they both are stumbling over how sorry they are, tripping over each other with more and more meaningless regrets. Their words tumble out in rapid succession, never reaching any point of contact, runaway trains outside their control.

"Of course I won't tell the doctors, Clarice. Really, it's fine.

What's wrong with resting? And you know the doctors would never object . . ."

"Just had to rest my feet a moment. A long day. I'm almost through out here, I'll get out of your way till you're done . . ."

For a moment both of them pause, and then Lucy remembers Clarice's advice to "plant your feet," and she thinks about asking her about this but isn't sure she should, and then Clarice is backing her cleaning cart down the hall, and Lucy picks up her address book and backs toward the door, and each of them keeps chattering politely, unheedingly, until the door closes between them and they stop at last. For a moment each woman gazes at the closed door in front of her and knows, just for that instant, that behind that door are entire worlds, held together by fragile threads that are fraying at the edges, worn from heat and overuse. Outside Lucy walks to the bus stop, and inside Clarice starts mopping the first examining room.

In another part of town, in the neighborhood by the tracks, Anthony Johnson dreams that he is walking down a row of prison cells, shining his flashlight into each one to check on the sleeping prisoners. In several of the cells he sees people he recognizes—kids he knew in school or on the neighborhood basketball court. Nothing about this is strange—it actually happens quite often at his job.

But when he shines his light into the last cell on the row, he sees his father curled up on the bunk. He is wearing his black Sunday suit. The light wakes him, and he looks up at his son and smiles tenderly. Then, pointing his finger at Anthony, he says something indecipherable to him, and then suddenly he is gone.

In the dream, Anthony knows his father has left out of disappointment in his son.

"Wait, Daddy," Anthony says. "I'll still make you proud, I promise."

He wakes to the roar of the 6:35 train, racing to Chicago behind his head. He knows that he'll never have a better life than his father if he stays in Michigan City. And he knows the trains are bound to stop running soon.

Several blocks away, Joey Christianson sits in front of the TV in his grandfather's old rocking chair. Lucy should have been home an hour ago, but he isn't surprised by how late she is. As he sits and sips his beer, staring blankly ahead, he is reliving, yet again, the waking dream that's haunted him since Lucy came to stay with him. It's the one where he struggles for hours to fix another broken-down Chicago and South Shore train, only to discover that it's the one that's going to take her away from him.

2. Baby

Baby Cox, singer with Duke Ellington's Orchestra in the twenties. All that guttural groaning, not even words.

You know what that was, what it is.

Shiny snail's trail along the inside of your thigh dries to a powdery dust. You have fucked a married man. After this, you think, there's no going back. The relief of knowing that tastes like rain.

Like something stuck in Baby Cox's throat almost, but what if it was never clarity she wanted anyway? She'd only laugh at that. Say something like, If you don't understand, baby, too bad for you.

This is somehow new and different, you know. The way you just bounded up from that bed and showered and hit the sidewalk almost flying. Call if you want to, I won't be waiting by the phone.

Years ago standing at a motel window, pulling back that god-forsaken, dust-dragging drapery and staring out at a parking lot full of American cars, you got a glimpse of this. That hazy mid-morning sun was making your stomach pitch, but still, for an instant, you could see a cleaner, sharper future.

Free of messy ties. Like that dream, the night before he left, of countless red Chinese jump ropes tied in a mass of intersecting lines across the bathroom floor. Put there as a trap, by him. "It'll keep the floor clean for a change," he said in the dream.

Your only regret is that he left before you could.

Now you'd be gone the next day. His stuff would never cross your threshold. "You'll have to keep it somewhere else, it'll keep this place clean for a change."

You planned to spend a week with another man that spring but cut it short when his other habits made the sex go limp. Don't kid yourself, you wanted to say, this isn't about anything else.

When a white man gets too full of his own semen-inflated self, mention black men you have known. There's no quicker way to deflate that sad skin-sack balloon.

And then those dreams, which you know have to be about your own body somehow. Pears turning ripe, too ripe before your very eyes. A lemon growing a conical lattice-work of mold from its end. So rapidly ripe they're almost rotten. Saying, if they used words, Do you dare to touch? Can you handle a smell that strong, that full of funk?

You wonder how you could have bought it all for so long. Always thinking, if you fuck me will you love me? Those years are a serious blot on your memory, but every clean escape burns a line right through the haze of all that wrong-headed need. In bed with a man now in the morning it gets hard to breathe, and the flight afterwards is almost better than all that came before.

Some people say you might regret this but you doubt it.

Part of why is that you like picturing your own death. Not the sorry mourners-around-the-hospital-bed scene of your youth. Just the way it seems like it might feel. You've dreamed that too. Lying on your stomach on the floor, a kind of meditation exercise that works almost too well: you feel what dying feels like. And it's perfect.

But only when you're ready for it. Only when you've earned it. In ways you're still trying to figure out. Sometimes by taking risks. Other times by locking the door and staying inside for days.

What you want, you know, is that thing that Baby Cox had going. Something without words, without pictures, without a name. Something in your blood like a drug, but there for free with the right combination. It's not your heart you want unlocked, that much you know for sure.

Can you stand the smell, the heat? Put your finger in the flame, right there in its center. Hold it there if you're so good.

There just aren't words for that. And no picture ever gets it right. All you can do is keep it up. Repetition might mean perfection, one day.

You'll keep on trying anyway.

The Slow and Painful Demise of the American Family

The call from Phoebe came less than an hour after I'd found Lester's letter—or rather my letter with Lester's colorful annotations—under my door. Generally I'm a sucker for coincidence, for any seeming glitch in boring, day-to-day predictability. But I had a little trouble keeping perspective on this one. Phoebe and Lester had thrown me a bit, making me more prone than ever to duck below the crossfire, seek the relative calm of the trenches.

But of course, everything was all of a piece, like it always is; nothing's ever really all that random. What I mean to say is the fact that Phoebe had been carrying around my phone number and I hers—a Brooklyn exchange that I only dialed twice—had to do with other things in my life. Like the fact that I was seeing someone again, a man named Keith, and we'd been together long enough to have toothbrushes in each other's apartments and for me to sleep, some nights, in one of his old T-shirts. And—I hate how familiar this all is, and what it says about the number of times I'd done this before—it also meant that the only messages on my answering machine in those days, besides the ones from Keith, were from my mother. That is, I'd done the usual slow and unobservable severing of ties with friends in the face of the tidal wave of romance—the predictable throwing overboard of excess weight, anything that would make me less seaworthy, less available for this man's affections.

And, true to form, once the sound of my toothbrush hitting Keith's medicine cabinet had prompted the usual panic reaction, leading him to suggest we not spend quite so much time together, I started casting about for women friends who might find me interesting and vice versa, kindred spirits with whom to while away the hours—and avoid too much close scrutiny of those hours—until Keith felt ready for another series of nights that would end with us in my bed or his.

Phoebe didn't really strike me as someone I'd care to get to know, frankly. And now, it stuns me to realize how little I knew about her, despite a movie or two and an occasional meeting for coffee. But then I'd never really thought of the YMCA as a likely place for making friends, or the fact that a woman was sweating away on the Stairmaster next to mine a sufficient reason to strike up a conversation that ended in an exchange of phone numbers.

I'd seen other women do it, though, and I figured I'd better start trying it out. I was thirty-five, which meant, of course, that all my old high school and college connections were rapidly disappearing (into suburban houses with baby nurseries). And the options at work were even worse: with me in the publications office of the small nonprofit agency I worked for were two sniping, middle-aged gay men and a twenty-year-old summer intern who rarely removed the headphones of her Walkman.

So a couple months before, when Phoebe and I found ourselves finishing our workouts and heading for the sauna at the same time, I took the plunge and complimented her on her sneakers—bright orange hightops with multicolored shoestrings. She wore these with frayed black tights that accentuated the boniness of her long, skinny legs. She wore bright red lipstick and her eyes, I noticed, seemed to focus rarely, if at all.

She was the kind of woman my mother would describe as "blowsy," a word I've always liked because its sound makes me think of folds of billowing white sheets blowing in a springtime breeze. And I suppose that's why I've always been rather drawn to the kind of people my bored and bitter mother would label with the term—though I've rarely sought them out as friends.

Maybe my mother does know best. It came to seem like a serious mistake to have ever pursued some kind of connection with a woman like Phoebe.

She seemed glad enough to talk to me, despite my conservative white sneakers and unassuming shorts and T-shirt. We had a reasonable, get-acquainted conversation in the sauna. I learned that she was a painter, living—"only for the moment"—in a friend's apartment in Brooklyn. She wanted to move out soon, she said, as soon as she got the money together for a deposit.

That's actually the most I ever learned about her.

We made plans to see a movie or something together, and I was rather taken aback when she called me the very next day, to ask if I'd like to get together that evening.

Taken aback but pleased, too, and I hate to admit why. That was during a particularly difficult time for Keith and me, and it pleased me to be able to tell him I couldn't see him that night, that I'd made plans with someone I'd met at the Y. I left the message on his machine, leaving the question of my new friend's gender and/or sexual orientation wide open. Let him think what he would, I decided.

These things work, that's the sad thing. Maybe I wouldn't have resorted to steps like that if they didn't really work.

So Phoebe came by my apartment, which is a nice one, I'll admit that. It's on a pretty, tree-lined street in Greenwich Village, just a block away from the Hudson River.

It was a gift from my guilty parents, who had sold our family house in the Jersey suburbs and bought a condo in Florida. To recompense my brother and me for selling off the family homestead—a house I lived in from age five until I left for college and that I did love dearly—they provided him with cash for a new wing on the smaller, but comfortable, house he shares with his family, also in the Jersey suburbs. And they gave me the money for the inside buyer's price for my apartment.

So at age thirty-five I owned a Manhattan apartment in one of the nicer neighborhoods in the city. This made quite an impression on Phoebe.

"Your own place!" she gushed when she came over that evening, and I tried to express appreciation of my good fortune. But I couldn't help letting some of my irritation about the whole arrangement slip.

"It's just not the same as a house, though, you know? I mean, I feel like I don't really have a home now that my parents sold the house. This is just a tiny one-bedroom apartment with bad closet space and a junky old kitchen."

That was one of the times when I noticed that strange, unfocused quality in Phoebe's expression as she stared at me, clearly not comprehending my disgruntlement.

I got nervous then, and I did what I always do when that happens—I started babbling on and on, creating, I could tell, even more confusion for poor Phoebe. "It's just that I always thought that when I was an adult—and I think being thirty-five means I'm pretty much there, don't you?—I always thought I'd live in a house like my parents' house. You know, lots of room, a nice yard, a garage, the whole thing. But instead all I have is this crowded, run-down place in the city, and now I can't even go to my folks' house to get away from it all. Unless I want to sit alongside the pool with all the retirees and sleep on the ridiculously uncomfortable couch they've got in that stupid condo now."

Fortunately we were running out of time. I say fortunately because Phoebe's expression wasn't changing in the least—she clearly wasn't getting it—and I don't think I realized at the time how close I was to a full-scale, bottom-dropping tantrum, aimed at pretty much everyone who mattered to me: my brother and his wife for having an actual house, however small; my parents for the sale of their—our—house; and Keith, frankly, for not yet having asked me to marry him.

But we had to race to make a 7:30 movie. On the way there,

Phoebe said to me, "Maybe you could have the kitchen redone or something. Maybe that would make it feel more like home."

It was Phoebe who suggested it first. Phoebe, of all people, who planted the seed that would lead to Lester's outburst on the day, a couple of months later, when Phoebe called me again.

That night after the movie I begged off having coffee and raced home to check the answering machine. Sure enough, the light was blinking. I knew it would be Keith.

I saw Phoebe once or twice after that, usually just for a quick drink or cup of coffee, always in my neighborhood. Keith and I started getting quite a bit cozier, and I just didn't have as much time for other plans. I tried a month or so later to call her, but when I dialed her Brooklyn number, the phone just rang and rang.

I wanted to tell her that I'd decided to follow her advice and have the kitchen redone, that I'd called someone to come and give me an estimate the next day. But when there was no answer the second time I dialed, I gave up. She'd probably suggest we get together if I reached her, I thought, and by that time I preferred to keep my nights open for Keith.

Keith was a lawyer, and that was kind of unusual for me. I'd generally dated more creative (not to say blowsy) types—actors, writers, musicians. I'd lived with a couple of people before I met Keith, but I didn't take those relationships very seriously. Then one day I saw my thirty-fourth birthday looming around the corner. I looked around me—at my apartment, my job, my life—and decided I didn't especially care for any of it.

It was right around that time that my parents turned our family house over to a set of strangers, dropped a check for the down payment on my apartment in my lap, and flew south, this time for more than just the winter. Not too long after that, I met Keith at a party.

I still have a bit of an impulsive streak at times. Or at least Keith seemed to think so. It wasn't his favorite thing about me. To be honest, I guess I thought it would impress him if I had my kitchen redone. The practicality of it, I mean, the way it seemed to say, "I can take care of myself; I can make this charming little Greenwich Village apartment into a home." Even though that wasn't what I felt at all. Even though Phoebe's suggestion about my kitchen had seemed laughably feeble to me at the time.

Two days before the workers were scheduled to begin their work, it occurred to me that maybe I should alert Lester about the noise. Lester, who lived right below me, was dying of AIDS. We'd never discussed this directly, but it was frighteningly obvious, as AIDS in the late stages always was. His lover Mark had died less than a year before. I had sent flowers and a card. What else could you do? What could ever possibly be enough?

I liked Mark. He and Lester were already living in the building when I moved in. Lester seemed quieter and moodier. We hardly ever talked.

So I wasn't prepared for his reaction to my note. Here's what I said:

Dear Lester,

I'm going to have some work done on my apartment, on the kitchen actually, that should last no more than a week. I'm concerned that the noise might bother you. I'll definitely make sure the work is done only during the day so it doesn't disturb your sleep; if you'll let me know what time you usually get up in the morning, I'll make sure the workmen don't start before that time.

Hope you're doing all right. Please let me know if regular working hours, say 9:00 to 6:00, are okay for the workmen.

Best,
Suzanne in 4C (243-0473)

I labored over that note for quite a while. In fact, Keith laughed at me for taking such a long time, for all my fits and starts.

Was it presumptuous even to ask, I wondered? Would he find it insulting? After all, I probably wouldn't have said anything at all to a healthy downstairs neighbor. Or would I? Should I have asked him long ago, before I'd lined everything up, if it would be a problem? And should I have offered more? Part of me wanted to say, "Please let me know if there's anything I can do for you," but it felt childish and gratuitous to do that. I never saw anyone who looked like family members going into Lester's apartment. But I did sometimes see friends. He appeared to have at least a few people looking after him.

Some of them were sick, too.

Keith shook his head and chuckled as I threw down my pen in frustration. "Poor little Suzanne," he said, "poor little Suzanne and all her moral quandaries."

Sometimes, when Keith said things like this, my stomach seemed to clench—a mini, internal alarm—and I wanted to say something bitter to him. In the past, with other men, that was what I would have done. It's what I saw my mother do, more times than I care to remember, with my father.

But by then I'd begun trying to hold my tongue. There was a second, more menacing alarm that seemed to go off when I thought of the possibility of losing Keith.

I slid the note under Lester's door that night, and when I got home from work the next evening, the same note was back, under my door. I'd tried to imagine all the ways Lester might respond. I knew I was probably being unrealistic, selfish even, when I imagined his voice on my answering machine, nearly overcome with gratitude, thanking me for taking the time to think of him. But nothing could have prepared me for what he did.

At first I thought he'd drawn me a colorful picture in response. I could see, through the folded paper, bold lines and shapes drawn in brightly colored ink—playful, summer-bright colors, grass green, sunshine yellow, rosy-cheeked pink.

I opened the page eagerly, anticipating a warm response, a loving pat on the head for my unusual thoughtfulness—the esteemed blessing of a peaceful, dying man.

It took a while for Lester's words to register. But at last it all came together, and my mind made the leap from the happy, loving words the bright colors had led me to expect, to the reality of what was actually there. Between the neat, carefully penned lines of my note, in bold, technicolor fury, Lester had written:

BOOM! She's dressed to kill, in her high heels again.

BOOM! She's slamming doors in peevish fury at her boyfriend.

BOOM! They've made up and now they're fucking wildly, the bedposts pounding ruthlessly against the floor and wall.

BOOM!

BOOM!

BOOM! Single life in the city!

Then, at the bottom of the page, he had scribbled, in plain old blue ballpoint:

> I don't give a damn what you do to your apartment. Rebuild the whole thing if you want, and do it whenever you want. What is driving me mad is the noise of your whole life, your relentless banging day in and day out.

Fortunately—or maybe unfortunately, I'm not sure—Keith was there when I read it. I fell apart, of course, and he held me for as long as he deemed appropriate, then gripped my shoulders and made me look at him.

"Suzanne," he said, "he's insane. He's dying of AIDS, and he's lost his mind. That happens to some people with AIDS, it just does. They lose all sense of proportion, they really do lose their minds."

I stared at him, and an interesting battle was waged, there and then, in my mind. It was a fairly familiar one, I realized. One side of my head said, "He's pretending to be an authority again, once again about something he knows absolutely nothing about. He's also being patronizing. Why would you let someone talk to you like that?"

But then the other side kicked in, a familiar side, one I'd known, really, all my life. It didn't say anything. It just acknowledged how nice it felt to have someone make it all better, make it all go away, say, "He's insane, Suzanne," or "I'll handle this, Suzanne," or "Come on, honey, you know I love you; why make it all so difficult?"

It was the siren song of marriage, the luring call of some wonderful, exotic drug, a father's voice, a husband's voice, saying here it all ends, here there is safety, and you can be a child, this will be home. Just stop fighting and you can have this blissful release, this end of strain and effort, this delighted letting-go into years of deep and dreamless sleep in a feather-soft bed in someone else's house.

It won. I decided Keith was right. There was nothing to be done, I'd made all the effort I could. Lester was crazy and that was too bad. But that's life for some people. What else could I do?

Keith said he'd take me out to dinner. A reward for such a quick, model recovery. But just as we were heading out the door, the phone rang.

It was Phoebe. She said she was at the Y. She said she really wanted to see me.

"Well sure, Phoebe," I said. "I've been wondering what you've been up to. But I can't come now. Maybe we could get together later in the week?"

This was a question posed to both Phoebe and Keith. I glanced in his direction as I asked it, my eyebrows raised question marks. Would it be all right if I made a plan without him? He shrugged, his signal for "We'll see." I'd have to work it all out later, I thought; the thing now was to hurry off the phone.

What was it that kept me from hanging up? I'm still not really sure. She sounded breezy and a little manic—too manic, actually—but I could've sworn I heard her swallow a sob when she said, "Well, I really kind of need to talk to you."

Keith was surprisingly understanding. "I'll just go up to my place, get some carry-out food and get a little work done. It'd probably do you good to go work out with her. You can just come up when you're done."

I had a hunch Phoebe didn't have a workout in mind, but because Keith had suggested it—had, in fact, told me it would be good for me—I grabbed my gym bag as I headed out the door.

When I reached the women's locker room, I was greeted by an unpleasant odor. Not the usual day-old sweat or the damp, mildewed smell of overused showers, but another smell that had become familiar to city dwellers by then—an old, tired, unwashed body smell. The smell of someone who'd been living on the streets. I remember thinking, Oh god, another homeless person has snuck in to use the showers.

It was Phoebe.

It was a hot, humid summer evening, but she was dressed in jeans and a sweatshirt, with a jacket over that. At her feet were three bulging shopping bags, filled with clothing and newspapers. I had an overwhelming impulse to run back out the door, but she had already spotted me.

She was sitting on one of the sofas in the central area of the locker room. Women in robes and towels were walking through, staring at her surreptitiously, giving her a wide berth. I didn't want to approach her. This was not someone you wanted to be seen talking to in such a public space. But I didn't have time to think of a way out. She was calling my name, waving to me frantically.

She stood up to come toward me, and I motioned her to sit back down. I took a deep breath, then walked over and sat next to her.

She was smiling uncontrollably, blinking her eyes at an unreasonable rate. Was she blinking back tears? Her hands fluttered from her lap to her shoes—the same orange hightops—then back to her legs, where she fiddled with the seam of her jeans.

"Phoebe," I finally said. "What's going on? I tried a while ago to reach you in Brooklyn, but no one ever answered." I stopped. Why was I explaining?

She giggled and grabbed a strand of hair, stroking it nervously, almost violently.

"Yeah, my friend got evicted." Another nervous, strangely husky laugh. "And I guess you could say I've worn out my welcome everywhere else. I've been sleeping in Tompkins Square Park with a group of people I sort of know. But it started to get a little uncomfortable."

She stared down at her feet, and I was glad because I wanted her to stop. I didn't want to know the rest.

"I'm not sure why you called me, Phoebe," I said. Suddenly I felt angry. I hardly knew this woman. How could I ever have guessed she was someone who could live this way, that she would end up homeless?

She must've read the expression on my face. Because it seemed as if she suddenly turned every bit as angry as I was. Her voice, which had been breathless and unnaturally cheerful till then, turned dark and deadly serious when she said, "I can tell I really scare you, Suzanne. I wonder what you're so afraid of?"

Then, just as suddenly, she went back to manic, nearly giddy. She pulled a plastic card out of her pocket. "So I'm going through my stuff today, and what should fall out but my old YMCA ID! It's expired, of course, but I knew the night guy never checked too closely. As a matter of fact, mine was expired for most of the time I was coming here! So I think, well, at least I can go have a shower. And then I looked closer and realized it had your phone number written on it."

She held it out, right in front of my eyes, her undeniable proof that we had, in fact, had some sort of connection once, however tenuous. We'd gone so far as to exchange phone numbers. But what did that mean?

I wasn't sure of social codes in such a situation. It was 8:00 at night. This woman had nowhere to sleep, and she had my phone number written on her ID card. Did that mean I should take her home? I recoiled at the thought—not of having Phoebe in my place (she'd been there before, after all), not of bringing the sights and smells of homelessness into the safe, clean domain of my charming West 12th Street apartment. What horrified me was the thought of Keith's reaction—how impulsive, alien, and threatening such a gesture would be to him.

"You know," she said, "they've got rooms here at the Y. They're twenty-five dollars a night, though."

A quick, easy solution—and one that made me look at least moderately compassionate, certainly more so than a lot of people, I thought. She'd barely uttered the price of a night's lodgings before my wallet was out of my bag.

"Phoebe," I said, doing my best to hide the giddy relief I felt, "why don't I come by and meet you here on my lunch hour tomorrow? Maybe we can talk then about what you might do next." This would give me time, I reasoned, to figure out what to do. Maybe make some phone calls, come up with some other options besides my own apartment.

She stared vacantly at me. Finally she nodded slowly. "Sure, Suzanne," she said, and I could've sworn I heard that same angry edge in her voice again.

I left then, practically running to the uptown subway, the one that would deliver me to the safe confines of Keith's apartment.

Subway time in New York. An unparalleled experience—one you won't get anywhere else. Usually there's too much happening, too much of a colorful parade of performers, beggars, sellers of cheap toys and watches through the cars to allow much time for reflection. But that night the ride up to Keith's was different. If there was a chorus of desperate voices on the train that evening, I didn't notice it. I was thinking, again, about Lester's letter.

I never wore heels, least of all in the middle of the night. I wasn't a door slammer; I was more of a pouting-in-my-room sort, always have been. And I had a platform bed that didn't budge; no posts at all, anywhere.

But I knew, then, what Lester meant. My everyday life was just that—everyday life. It was as mundane as the next guy's, and its absolute normalcy screamed at Lester, bruising his faltering body with the bellowing of ringing telephones, cooking meals, easy movement from room to room, a shared bed. The hushed soundlessness of sleep deprived him of sleep of his own. I'm not sure why, but I understood that then.

And I knew he was right; it was utterly, unspeakably unfair that he'd been denied such things. But what could I do? What could anyone do?

Things like this never happened in the suburbs, I thought, without a trace of irony. In our lovely old Victorian on a scenic green lawn, the only things below us, listening to our lives upstairs, were the melodious crickets in the basement.

When I got to Keith's, he was immersed in a Mets game on the television, and I was glad. If he'd tried to touch me then, I don't know what I would have done. At that moment, I wouldn't have been able to bear the feel of his skin against mine. I went straight to bed and fell immediately into a deep sleep.

The next morning at work I made a few calls to some social service agencies. One suggested a women's shelter (one I'd read a scathing exposé of in the paper the week before); another said if Phoebe came in person—to the Bronx—she could be put on a waiting list for an SRO. Those were the helpful ones.

I considered trying to reach her family, but I didn't even know her last name. Finally, though, I settled on this plan for my meeting with her: I'd try to get her to give me the name of someone, anyone, in her family. I'd tell her I would try to track this person down, make the phone call for her, try to explain her circumstances. After all, I thought, things like this *were*, ultimately, the family's responsibility. If not her family, who else?

If that didn't work, I didn't know what I'd do. I had no back-up plan when it came to the slow and painful demise of the American family.

My body felt heavy and lumbering as I walked the ten blocks to the YMCA in the noonday sun. When I reached the lobby, Phoebe was nowhere in sight. She wasn't in the locker room, either.

I sat down to wait in the lobby. At one o'clock, when there was still no sign of her, I headed to the desk to ask about her. No one by that name had checked in the night before, they said. And no one who looked like Phoebe had turned in a key that morning.

Instead of going back to work, I walked home slowly, casting furtive glances at all the dark, shadowy figures that curled inside doorways or lay sprawling, sound asleep, on the sidewalks. Had there always been this many? When had I stopped noticing? I expected every ragged body to be Phoebe, every set of hands as twitching and nervous as hers, every pair of eyes as lost in an overheated cloud of confusion.

At home I called the office to say I was sick, then dialed Keith's number at work.

"Well, I guess she had a good time on you. Wonder how much heroin you can buy with twenty-five dollars?"

"You're a lot of help, Keith," I snapped, forgetting myself for a moment.

"Okay, I'm sorry. Maybe she put the money to good use. You know, she might be schizophrenic or something, Suzanne. That's not something you can tell right away, especially when the person's medicated. She's probably off her medication, and not the least bit interested in having a steady home. Those people go their own way. Even their own families can't control them.

"Hey," his voice went soft and suggestive, "why don't you just crawl under the covers and take a good long nap. You need to rest, just get your mind off all this craziness. I'll pick up a nice bottle of wine after work, we'll have a good dinner. And then I'll help you relax even more . . ."

Then soft laughter. I could picture the curl of his lip right then, the gleam in his eye. The drug kicked in again, starting, as it often did, below the belt. That soft, seductive hypnosis—a male voice promising comfort without care.

When I hung up, though, my eyes came to rest on Lester's letter, there on the table next to the phone, where I'd left it the night before when Phoebe called.

I stared at the letter, watching the multicolored BOOMs flow together in hazy pools of color—like little oil slicks pulsing on the page—through the film of my tear-filled eyes. Suddenly I realized why those colors had seemed so familiar to me. They were the same Crayola crayon colors I had used when, as a child, I drew my favorite picture, of the house I would live in one day. A big square house with a sloping green roof, under an orange sun bursting with beams in a cloudless, bright blue sky. A large front door in the center, two perfectly square windows, with pretty pink curtains, on either side. And outside the house, standing under a brown-trunked, green-leafed tree, were four stick figures, two tall and two short, mom and dad and girl and boy. Four stick figures with wide, thin smiles and empty-circle eyes, frozen and still, staring out at the nothingness, waiting for something to happen.

I made one more phone call then, to cancel the work on my kitchen, which was scheduled to start the next morning. Then I took Keith's advice and crawled under the covers, buried myself in the soft white folds of sheets and pillows, waiting, though it's true I knew better, for something to happen, for some kind of springtime, back-yard breeze to carry us all away.

Tell Me Everything

CITY

There was a young woman standing and crying in the rain outside a bank in a suburb. It's a suburb that's gone, just dropped off the map as I see that place now, but for purposes of comparison it's important to know that at that point I did not even know to call it a suburb.

It was a world to itself with a map all its own and it was only later that I came to lose myself in the map of what came below it, that is, to the south.

But the girl in the rain—there's a reason for her to move to this other grid because sometime later, at the heart of this other map, I would stand in the rain in a borrowed dress and high-heeled shoes and remember how I'd seen her that day, standing there and crying in the rain.

I'd be weaving a bit from alcohol, standing there at dawn trying the find my keys. The man in the car behind me was a writer and for some hours we had been talking, only talking, and drinking, where he lived at a point farther north, though not so far north as the suburb that before I hadn't recognized as one.

When I saw her what I thought was, "That could be me," though I don't know that I ever cried that way in the rain and later, a little south, I rarely cried. I mainly spat in fury, wondered why I'd worn a borrowed dress, thought of how little it had really gotten me after all.

There is a story that I wanted to tell later, and it radiates from somewhere else on that city map, to the south and to the west, where the blocks and buildings teem and other verbs like that—short, dense verbs of one syllable, implying maybe dark. Loud. Colorful, and a little poor perhaps.

I saw these teeming blocks in slower motion than I might have, gradually coming in to them on the back of a motorcycle. And yes, it was as romantic as that sounds; we were not even wearing helmets, even though elsewhere on that map (and certainly on others) such recklessness would be an awful crime.

The story was about a young woman whose mother slams the door as she leaves her daughter's apartment, distraught, in tears—it seems they're almost fighting for some man. In the story she is more heroic than her daughter's ever been. In the story she drives away from the teeming blocks to the south and west in the city, drives south into the country over highways that splinter off fan-like, like the lines, my story goes, on the palm of a woman's hand.

Looking back I make a map. From here I think I see some juncture, node—some swelling in the narrow trail where a man on a motorcycle appears.

Maps, and grids of other sorts. Vast hollow buildings, all windows. Parking garages, train tunnels, everything a part of some confoundedly orderly arrangement that's planned so much, so far, you could consider it out of control.

One night at the earlier center of that city map I found myself face-to-face with the towering structure of my childhood dreams. An empty building, a highrise full of hollow apartments, still being constructed. There was a rickety, plywood elevator there at the side with plastic sheeting flapping in the fierce fall wind off the lake. I thought to myself, this is ominous somehow. I thought it should be in a story, about how when a woman knows she's going to leave the man on the motorcycle with all the books on film and the dark and teeming friends, it feels to her as if she's swallowed something whole and heavy. About the way, at a moment like that, that plywood elevator made perfect sense and I only wanted to ride it then, ride it far past the distant top of that high and empty shell.

I didn't cry then, either. I was always planning instead, I was always shaping other grids.

I could tell you more, for instance, about the story of the daughter and her mother who slammed the door and ran across the street on one of the dense and teeming blocks. How naïve that story was, but striking too. How the mother driving on roads that spread like veins, like lines in skin, was the only restful moment and it came at the very end. And you could say that it was very sad, the way she'd stumbled down the stairs and out the door to her car. I don't recall if it was raining.

The girl in the rain in the suburb was named Sarah, and she wore a long man's trenchcoat, open and hanging limp and lifeless at the front and nothing on her head. This meant she was wet, her exposed T-shirt soaking at the front and water streaming from the sodden strands of her long brown hair.

There wasn't much money in her bank account, and she had a sense that she was living life wrong. That is, it seemed that she did not know how to play by the rules of romance and the only men she noticed were those who tended not to see her most of the time.

She was a student at the university in the suburb and she thought she'd like to leave but that seemed unlikely, as it was one of the few maps that she knew. It looked like she was crying, but really, in rain like that, how would you truly know?

Later, she would be in the city to the south, on a street with high, hollow buildings and the right amount of quiet space between everyone at all times, standing in the predawn light in a borrowed dress and heels and fumbling for her keys, weaving from far too much alcohol and distraught about the writer who had brought her there.

If you don't want me, why not?

She was very careful not to stumble on the stairs because maybe, just maybe, he might be out there watching.

I was a long way then from the woman who stumbled down the stairs and out the door and to her car and drove on roads that spread like channels on the underside of a leaf. A long way, yes, but also only around 20 blocks north and 12 blocks east. Maps give one perspective—what's a lifetime in those squared-off terms?

I rode west on the back of a motorcycle, hair streaming behind, watching how the buildings changed from quaint to worn with work. In the middle of that journey was a foundry, a throwback to the old days of the city, stubbornly digging in its heels and smelting its steel in vast, hot drums. We rode by slowly and I stared at the seething. It felt like some hellish, centripetal center, as if all roads were pulled to its middle and poured like liquid into its vats. Men with cigars stood and watched.

This was not the way I'd learned to see a city. We rode on, and the buildings had worn paint, and sometimes sofas and whole families on the front porch. The air smelled of mold and of life being lived there, and the signs above bars and bakeries were in Spanish or Polish.

Here is where my story may be most ingenuous, even naïve. About the young woman's delight in the blending of cultures, how she sometimes thought of her desire to cross those lines as a fundamental virtue. But really, we do talk as if that's noble—brave and noble to mix with others whose skin is darker than our own, with no immediate plans to colonize.

Would my reader want to know that the man on the motorcycle had skin that was darker than mine? Could I make some poetry of the way, without trying, our faces made a patterned play of light and shadow? If I ask instead of tell it, does that make me seem sincere?

I had a job. It wasn't one I particularly enjoyed, and that made me feel more at home in this city where work has a history more visible than it sometimes is. This was a time of sexual awakening for me, if you want to know that version of the truth, and I had the time and inclination to concentrate on that then.

We met at a street fair east of him but west of me. He smiled at me and, well, I felt that smile rush right to the lower regions of my body. We were lovers very quickly, and it was a motorcycle ride without a helmet.

But nothing lasts forever, though that girl in the rain outside the bank in the suburb could very well still be there. Who can say what progress has truly been made? When you ride the elevated train in that city, you rarely get the sense of the overall pattern of the thing; you cannot see yourself from outside, traveling with some kind of surety from there to here.

I think that's why I always dream of trains. Of leaving something behind and trying to get back on, but never getting it quite right, never quite the same again—the thing I left gone for good.

The mythos of cities. In the end perhaps I might be the older woman who stumbles on the stairs. I'd like to stumble and not give a damn, simply not give a damn who sees me fall.

One morning Sarah woke to the smell of frying bacon from the apartment below. She was sore and bleeding slightly, her mouth parched and tasting of cigarettes.

(That may be too many physical sensations at once. I don't recall the order in which I felt them, but chances are they weren't as simultaneous as that sounds.)

She found a T-shirt and her underwear, then her clothes—skirt, understated knit blouse, opaque pantyhose, shoes with subtle heels—in the neat pile where she'd left them in the corner. Had she really driven all this way just to have that happen? Just to lose her virginity to someone she used to know who was gone now, had been gone for a good long time?

She had a headache. That much is certain.

She didn't like it but she realized that she wanted coffee and another cigarette. How old am I? she asked herself; it was a favorite game of hers. Twenty-two or twenty-three? She was delighted when she didn't know for sure.

Either way, she thought, too old to have driven all this way for this. She walked out to go to the bathroom, and someone she didn't know was sleeping on the couch.

This was another university town, several hours away from the suburb to the north. She could get in her car now and drive somewhere for breakfast, but she could never seem to master this town's map somehow. All those one-way streets. Her head hurt and her stomach pitched a little.

It would be better to walk, she decided, so she did. At a coffeehouse called The Runcible Spoon she sat at a little table by a window and looked out at the rain. But she didn't cry.

She drank her coffee and decided to drive back to the suburb to the north. He had things to do, and she couldn't grasp the map of this town. It was not permitted for her to stay, that's how it seemed to her.

TOWN

When she was a child Sarah gazed at herself in the mirror in the girls' bathroom at her brand-new school and thrilled herself with the realization that she did not recognize herself in that image.

She was living in a very small town, the county seat of an agricultural county, and when she went to school it was a church-affiliated one, Lutheran, and they began each day with memory work—Bible verses first, eventually Luther's Small Catechism.

The Office of the Keys and the Confession, for instance, and several different creeds. And the books of the Bible, in order, which she can still rattle off at parties, especially if she's a little drunk.

It's a lovely story, really, how a girl like Sarah grows up and becomes someone who moves to New York City. At least it can be, and she is careful to try to tell it that way most of the time.

A girl who grows up.

There is one Bible passage, the one assigned to her at her confirmation (not chosen by her—that's not how these things work), and unfortunately it continues to haunt her despite her best efforts to grow up:

"I am the Vine, ye are the branches. He that abideth in me and I in him, the same bringeth forth much fruit. For without me, ye can do nothing."

From time to time Sarah has taunted herself with "For without me ye can do nothing," maybe because she's grown so used to being tortured by it that she would miss it if it were gone? She's never known for sure.

Once when Sarah was five, her neighbor, Jack Brown, who was fourteen, asked her to go for a walk with him and she did. And she didn't tell her parents. They walked to the town swimming pool and stood at the fence and watched the people inside for a while and then they walked home. And when they got there Sarah's mother was frantic—"We didn't know where you'd gone!" And she punished Sarah, making her stay indoors for several days, which baffled Sarah, though her strongest feeling by far was deep, inconsolable remorse over having worried her mother. She cried and cried, until her mother looked a bit alarmed.

Usually, she cried only in private, in her room with the door closed, and she stopped immediately if her mother knocked. Sometimes she would sneak outside on rainy days in the summer, and walk through puddles in the gravel drive in her bare feet.

DREAM

Don't bother bringing a compass here. Roads you think you know will simply drop away—turn from rock to fine, fine powder, air-borne dust rising 'round your feet.

A woman is buried under the shifting sand behind the tennis courts, asking in a small, hesitant voice for help. Another woman, terribly fat, is there with you, and it's as if her bulk has made her feel helpless; she tells you to go into the supermarket on the hill (where the high school should be) to ask for help. But the only people who could help, the only men that is, are the manager and his stock boy, and they both remind you of the nasty Afrikaner in a film you saw recently. So you leave without asking and when you get back to the shifting sand the fat woman has left, gone back to her office to work, you suppose, and so you squat and simply talk with the buried woman, about all kinds of things, and she sounds very, very tired.

Consider the map of a tennis court. Two distinct sides, perfect rectangles, with a clearly defined barrier, though it's only a net with holes (small ones, though, ones no ball could make it through). And on the sides, alleys—regions you may only enter if you are a twosome, a double, a couple of sorts.

In school I played strictly singles. In towns to the south of us, closer to the reach of the money from the river, I played on clay, the fine gray dust in spinning clouds around my bandaged foot.

"You drag your foot! What do you expect?"

And it's true, there is a neat round hole at the top left corner of all my discarded right sneakers. This could be a mark of some deep flaw in me, I think; here is where I wear my sin and always fail to rub it well away.

Most dreams happen behind the tennis courts, where you add a broiling river, wide and deep with rocky falls. Walk far enough and there's a castle of sorts, home of some crusty old Irish poet who offers you a photograph of yourself fifty or more years before and blesses you in a literary way. At the very back of his castle there is a straight cliff down; beyond that only angry waves as far as the rapidly moving eye can see.

You walk to the rocky beach behind the tennis courts but you are going against traffic; everyone's coming back to avoid the storm above the broiling river. They don't warn you not to go; they act, in fact, as if you are not there, all these people you knew in school who have children in their arms and hands and are wearing high-heeled shoes. Which strikes you as odd for the beach.

You know that they're only doing what you always asked them to, ignoring you that way.

I could place the girl in the rain any number of places on this landscape (I was wide awake when I saw her that first time), but I think I'd like her to be there in that storm above the broiling river. But if you'll permit me (you will—you are dreaming) I believe I'd like the river now to be behind a farmhouse that has burned, leaving only the cellar and foundation, and some lovely charred brick walls. Crying there, at that farmhouse several miles from the campus, in the growing storm.

And the woman who stumbles, now she'll be where I last saw her, rising from her bed in an absurdly lavish room in an inn in Massachusetts—rising from her bed and feeling her legs give way, stumbling, falling against the table by the bed, knocking over the tray that's there, the tray with a glass decanter and a half-filled glass.

Is she drunk? you ask.

That will certainly have to be decided. Is she the girl in the rain years later, stumbling in her drunkenness? Or the girl's mother, her legs giving way at the memory of something about her daughter (something to do with a man?), rising from the bed to dress herself and gather her bag and her car keys and run down the stairs and slam the door behind her?

And then what? There is no street to cross here, there is only a narrow country highway, and in Massachusetts there is no room for roads to fan in quite the way they do in Illinois.

She must not be that mother. There is a logic here, you have discovered, one that far exceeds the straight-line grid of maps. You play singles here, but you go into the alleys if you want. Think of all those dreams of walking, simply walking, from one end of a city to the other, as if any city ever had an end.

TOWN

They might have walked on Elm Street, across Walnut then Spring and then turning to walk down Bridge, their backs to the church behind them on the hill, ambling down the gradual slope to the swimming pool. Just below it was the town park—baseball diamond, small brown pond with ducks. And beyond that, behind the park and the high school tennis courts that were next to it, a mysterious ravine that seemed to Sarah deeper than it truly was—deep and hopelessly tree- and shrub-choked.

You could get so lost there, you could sink deep into that mud in your bare feet. She closed her eyes and tried to shake her fear away.

But it's possible—and somehow this seems right—that they didn't walk on Elm Street, did not take the nice route to Bridge Street and amble down the hill, the way Sarah would always walk when she went to the pool years later.

It may be that they walked down Bloomington Road, past the public school, past the basketball courts (were boys playing there without shirts, their blue jeans riding low on their hips?). Down still farther to the streets whose names she doesn't remember, crowded with rusted cars and small, angry houses that drew up right on their edges. It may be that Jack Brown wanted to walk this way, wave hello to friends he knew, see who was at the basketball courts.

Then they would have been near the Jay-C store parking lot (old-fashioned Coke machine in the corner by the first aisle, the bottles always sticking). This was almost—but not quite—all the way to Ewing, Sarah's town's "twin," as it was known. Though there wasn't much resemblance.

It may well be that Jack Brown preferred to walk this way to the swimming pool.

Years later—many years, when she no longer walked to the swimming pool—Sarah always walked to Ewing. She hoped for drunken factory workers, hoods on bikes. She tried to make her face look mean. It wasn't where her mother would have wanted her to walk.

Be back before dark, okay?

Okay.

What happens in Ewing after dark? What's so frightening there?

If they walked down Bloomington Road and onto the streets whose names Sarah did not know, they would have turned eventually and still crossed Walnut and Spring to Bridge. All different there, though; all much closer to Ewing. A meat packing plant. A canning factory, paper mill. Big cars crowding the houses, snarling dogs. A railroad track now out of use.

But when Sarah walked with Jack Brown it would have still been in use, littered with long and shiny flattened pennies. That kind of weight and heat brings out a strange kind of shine.

Her bathing suit was pink. Why did she have it on if they did not mean to swim?

* * *

Sarah sits in the pew and she is very quiet and good. Her coat is pink and her mother made it; it matches the dress she wears below it. In church everyone keeps their coat on. She is very quiet and good.

She stands when they all do, holds the hymnbook like she is reading it and singing along. She is thinking of the bathroom downstairs, the one marked "Girls" because they still have school in the church then, in three big rooms. The new building will not be ready until Sarah is going into the first grade.

In the church in the bathroom marked "Girls" there is a long wooden box, coffin-like, with flat green vinyl cushions atop it and this is where Sarah would like to be now. Lying on the cool green cushions, rising off the box and lifting its lid to peer inside.

Her mother will be in one of the stalls, the second one where the toilet is higher, and soon they will have to go back.

I thought you said you had to go.

I thought I did, I really thought I did—I felt something warm on my leg, I thought I was having an accident.

Sarah could lie on the green cushions in the old bathroom there for hours. Just lie there talking to her mother.

Let's never go back, let's stay here.

Silly girl.

She is told that when she was an infant she screamed as if in agony and terror the moment they entered the church. So much so that for weeks her mother had to stay home with her on Sunday mornings.

Let's not go back up there. Let's just stay here.

Stay here in the Girls room. Stay right here. Here in Girls.

Silly.

She felt something warm on her leg.

I have to go to the bathroom!

It will mean walking out in front of everyone. It will mean not sitting and being very quiet, very good.

But it won't last long and then we'll be there. I may be sick, it may be that I'm sick. I need to go to the Girls room.

The wooden doors on the stalls made a certain deep, groaning sound as they opened and closed. Deep enough to sound almost human. Deep and moaning with being that old and empty.

She can hear it very clearly, always, still.

DREAM

It's as if you're being forced to watch a movie. There comes a moment, always, when you say, I have to go, I can't watch any longer, you simply cannot make me see this.

It seems almost like England, but perhaps it's Massachusetts. That mist that's hanging in the air, maybe, and the fact that she is standing in a garden. She has her gardening tools.

This is lovely, but in a way that can only happen here. That is, it's gray and damp and filmy, but there is something ghostly and beautiful about that, and the flowers, which seem to be purple things on tall stems, irises perhaps, are so deeply, richly purplish-blue that blue could almost be a verb.

The flowers blue in this liquid gray garden. The flowers have blued again, here in this dream.

The woman could be any age but make her a bit older now. She is hiding here, maybe against her will. Her children are inside, she thinks. Or are they elsewhere, very very far away?

He has come to ask her what she is doing in such a place. And then we see (those of us who are watching, maybe against our will) that in truth it isn't quite so nice. The building, for instance, is bland and barracks-like.

Somehow we know that inside there all the people are old. Except her children. But where are her children?

She steps up from her weeding to face him, wipes away strands of hair with the back of her wrist; in her hand she has a small pruning shears.

She does not get a chance to answer.

Now he has the pruning shears and he's stabbing her, but not in the heart. He is raping her with the pruning shears, or trying to it seems, but he isn't really watching what he's doing, his aim is off and he's jabbing at her pelvis but above the slit he surely must be seeking.

This is when you say you have to turn away but of course it's already too late and of course this is why you did not want to watch in the first place.

Then you are driving with him in his car and together the two of you laugh about the time he did that. To you.

The flowers continue to blue, you assume. And the woman, somehow she does not die, she does not even bleed. Later, though, at dusk, she rises from her bed in her absurdly lavish room (too many things, clutter everywhere, she can't breathe from it all, it's stifling, all of it, there may not be any air left for her to breathe) and her legs give out beneath her, buckle like some flimsy colt's, and down she goes, dragging the tray with the glass and the decanter along with her.

She thinks, But I'm not this old. She has forgotten what he has done to her. And it's true, she may have been drinking.

Outside there is a road that leads away from the place, but she has forgotten all about that.

CITY

The way I'm telling it you'd almost think these maps were of something other than places. Or some other places. Places being something other than town or city or menacing ravine.

Once we rode together through the steel mills to the south and east. Desperate, rotting old things. Nothing works like it used to. And there was one whole brewery, one vast thing slowly peeling away in the sun and the rain, just left there empty and alone.

Even with a helmet, I saw it all or thought I did. These were great excursions into new terrains—wild culture safaris. I could have lived my whole life and never seen these things.

But we were only going to the beach—a crowded one, with those godawful factories still in sight far down the horizon and I thought I could maybe even smell them in the lake.

In those days I'd swim in anything. My ears hurt after but I contracted no serious diseases that I know of.

When we speak of disease now we should try to say what it is that we mean. Because here is something that we have to mean, and call it truth. Two young men I will forever associate first with small towns like the one I knew, and then with cities, are dead now. Dead and buried.

One, the last time I saw him, reached his hands over my eyes from behind and said, Guess who. Laughing, he said, Tell me about Chicago, tell me everything. He was small, like a little boy.

Tell me everything.

I have met a man who rides a motorcycle but I still fold my clothes in a neat little pile, no matter what. When we were in New York, that silly group of us for a week, we were only children and we still are. I don't know what to tell you about Chicago. I'm trying to see it but it's hard when you are there inside the thing.

He tried too, and now he's dead.

No, you do it, you tell *me* everything. Please tell me.

The last time I saw him he probably was not yet twenty.

Here may be why I can't stop dreaming of empty buildings. It's as if a whole city has been annihilated and all that is left standing on this scorched field is the empty shell of a tall building like you would see in a city, if there were one anymore. These dying boys, they leave you hollow.

DREAM

You are in the old Girls bathroom in the church and there is a problem with stains on your clothing. You don't see how you can go back.

Outside, they've all ordered a pizza. Your brother has asked through the door if you'd like any but you are ashamed and say no even though you are starving.

Positively starving.

But there is the problem of the stains, and really, you think, they would prefer you did not come out at all, asking as you always do for food.

DREAM

Neighborhoods get confused. You could be in the first city or the second, both have those vast avenues, blaring gasps of salsa or rap, smell of stale beer and dust. You only know you're walking and this could go on for days.

But then it's that town again, that senseless town that's built on squares, only now you've got some dry cleaning slung over your shoulder and heels that click on the pavement, and what should have been the Nazarene church on Main Street has become some kind of luxury hotel. And for some strange reason you are staying there, in your lovely heels and a suit that must be made of silk.

But you will not call home. You'll have dinner alone in the restaurant across the street, where the courthouse should be though now it looks more like the block across from Lincoln Center. It will surely be absurdly overpriced but you'll sit there by yourself with a book and you will not remember the Nazarene church (someone's wedding, all the girls with long hair; maybe the bride was pregnant; she always clicked her gum next to you in study hall) and you will do your best to overlook any traces of the courthouse there on the main town square. And you will not call home.

CITY

I went back for a meeting in a nice hotel. Twice. The first time I called the man on the motorcycle, went dancing, wore my wildest clothes, thought to myself that lives/cities/worlds were really all one. Found my way around with little trouble, rode in cabs. The second time I mainly sat in my room and stared out the window at the sun setting and all those snaking train tracks. Just stared there from my seat on the bed. No motion. I couldn't understand the grid, though I liked it somehow.

Tell me everything.

Maybe it was just a tinted window (isn't that always how it turns out) but the sky always looked hazy in an urban sunset kind of way, and there were more trains than I ever would have, than you ever would have, imagined. Trains gliding along like long slow snakes in a brown-gray haze, coming in and going out, and I thought I could have sat and watched for days. Never leaving that room.

I wish it were more exciting. What else would you like to know?

In the story, the daughter stares for what seems like hours at a woman braiding her daughter's hair, just watches her thick hands at work (they remind the daughter of her grandmother's German peasant hands—that's what she calls them, but how accurate is it to call someone a peasant now?).

In reality, I watched a woman braid her own rich, dark hair by herself, just reach around and make a perfect braid in three or four quick strokes, and it wasn't through a window, she was right there in front of me. On a train platform. In a different city.

Pardon all the trains, but that's the way these things go, and I'm not sure there's much I can do about that aspect of industrial development, and anyway, aren't those trains evocative? Even though I put the mother in a car. Had her run across the street—crying, upset, maybe something about a man (on a motorcycle, skin a shade too dark?)—and get into her car and drive south on roads that fan out like the lines on a woman's palm. A peasant woman's palm.

She was wiser in the story. But the grandmother may have been the wisest of all. That may be our biggest fear and our greatest (and most ridiculous) hope: that the older ones are always right.

But then what about the one who steps from her bed in that cluttered, overdone room in an inn in Massachusetts, steps up and immediately falls, maybe from alcohol? Some people don't get it right with age perhaps. She could be Sarah, me. The mother. The woman in the garden. If she'd gotten her life right, would she stumble? Would there even be the hint of a possible addiction? That kind of marking, branding, distinct coloration (flushed face), flaw?

But don't forget the gardening shears. And no, I still don't know where her children are. If they even are.

DREAM

Mark is driving some silly teenage kind of car, maybe a Trans Am, and he picks you up and there's a silly little dog peeking out of the glove compartment and you hold him on your lap. And together you drive to a restaurant (there in that town, the first town, the one made up of squares except for the ravine behind the tennis courts)—Polynesian theme, cheap beads hanging in the doorways, but they say the food is good. Only it's no longer Mark, it's Rob.

At last word, they'd both tested negative.

Tell me everything.

At the restaurant, you aren't sure who you're waiting for. It's just you and the dog now; Mark and Rob are gone.

TOWN

On the outskirts, the roads don't run in such straight lines. Until you get to the inevitable Lutheran church. Where order is restored. Go to the first row of the cemetery, turn right, just beyond the first pathway you'll see it: some relative's grave. Face west and you can watch the sun set behind that huge white cross above the brick of the church. Face east and the roads spread out in uniform lines and meet at corners like a military crease.

The only sound is the wind. If I were to lie down on the ground above that relative's grave I doubt he'd speak to me. We're quiet in my family; I really don't have much to say is what we're prone to say.

DREAM

You know you're going to be late for church, even if you leave the shopping mall right now. But still you stop for a donut, because at least you'll have the comfort of something sweet to eat.

On the way you drive your car off a bridge and into a small lake. Now you're really in trouble. Now you're really going to be late.

TOWN

Sarah has ridden her bicycle to Ewing. Don't tell anyone. She wants to see the shiny pennies on the tracks. Someone should have told her that the passenger trains stopped running there a long time ago. Now it's only an occasional freight and if there aren't people involved, what's the point of going to the railroad tracks? Where's the thrill in industrial transport?

She'll try the brickyard next. Scare herself at the thought of the heat inside those kilns. A few years from now she'll realize that this is the place where teenagers park their cars at night. The heat that makes a brick will be a lovely metaphor that she can put into a story and that way it will be a quaint truth that's all her own. Never mind if she can't find any pennies on the tracks, never mind if the kilns still scare her.

The ravine behind the tennis courts is not all that far away. And just up the road is the Lutheran church and the new school, just beyond the cemetery where she once was scolded for riding her bike with her friends and causing a ruckus. For being disrespectful of the dead in their tidy graves.

Down the hill is Ewing (poorer, houses crowding up against the streets, big barking dogs). There, no one will yell at her for riding her bike and making noise. But there she won't make noise, because her riding there is secret.

In between there is a deep ravine. Mud so thick and brown, she thinks, she could sink right down and never come back up. If you asked her about it—said, "Really, Sarah, would that be so bad?"—she'd give it some thought and probably say she didn't know.

Years later, in a room filled with carved wood and slightly tarnished silver and a glass decanter by the bed, if you asked the woman gripping the table to steady herself, she would also surely say she doesn't know. She could draw you a perfect map of the town: church, school, cemetery at the top of the hill; tennis courts and then ravine; factories and bars and small untidy houses at the base.

I would probably say, It's true that once you're sinking it's quite freeing. But nonetheless I'd want to leave things out.

You tell *me* everything. Not about the city, tell me about the town. Tell me why you had to leave. Tell me why, so I don't get stuck in this old-folks'-wisdom, watch-out-for-the-mud, bury-your-dead-in-neat-rows-with-white-stones quicksand.

There's always a risk of that. But if I give in, what do I do with deaths that aren't so tidy?

Sarah had two children but they all lived together in an old folks' home that looked like a barracks; and even there she couldn't escape that inevitable scene in the movie, the one where the man, invariably, rapes the woman—no matter how bad his aim is. One day I woke up and stumbled out of bed, nearly spilling the whiskey in the decanter by the bed; later I realized that what I tripped on were my stylish pumps; the silk suit that was just dry-cleaned lay crumpled in its plastic on the floor where I'd thrown it. My mother was right and so was my grandmother; everyone older than me was right (the crusty old Irish poet, for instance). I'm not sure what about, but surely they were right; the man on the motorcycle, for instance—really, what was the point of that?

* * *

I'm every bit as frightened as you are that it might not all turn out in the end. That is, that it might just make a turn, but not turn out. Just turn west, or south, down some side street, onto an unmarked exit ramp. And then just keep on going.

The mother is the one who keeps repeating "I am the Vine" and "Without me you can do nothing," and if Sarah thinks she's right, that is, if I think she's right, I couldn't even have started this, much less found a way to make a turn.

But the grandmother, she's different somehow. Her hands could be called peasant hands—with no apologies—because she did indeed work that hard. "He promised me we'd get off the farm, he was going to be a teacher, and I married him and found my head right back in a tomato pail." Pulling more things off of vines.

Besides agriculture there was house cleaning all those years. Not just her own—other women's, too. Not long before she died, she said, "You do what makes you happy." What's the point of looking for the point of the man on the motorcycle? was what she meant, I assume.

In the story I thought I wanted to tell, the one where the woman braided her daughter's hair in a window and later the mother drove south on roads that branched like the lines on a woman's palm, Sarah's grandmother worked in a photocopying shop, with big old outdated machines—ones that required her to feed each sheet one by one. I saw one like this once. The paper rested on a glass hump, like a little hill, with a rubber cover that you pulled over top. When the grandmother held it in place the weird green light of the machine lit up the veins on her peasant woman's hands—hands that were now feeding paper to a machine, endlessly multiplying other people's words.

She could have been right. She was very, very tired, and that may make you right.

The woman in the absurdly lavish room? It's funny, I know, but that room has to be inside the bland and barracks-like building, the old folks' home, for all of this to fit together. It would be nice if she were jumping up too fast because she heard her baby crying, but in truth, I'm afraid she is simply drunk. Or very, very tired. Or both.

Tell me everything.

The garden? Well, a place with rooms like that *would* have that kind of garden, wouldn't it? Oversized and richly colored flowers that do not quite seem real. More made up, more fantasy than anything. What's she doing in an old folks' home, anyway? Is she really all that old? There's her suit there on the chair, her low-heeled pumps kicked carelessly to the side. For all you know she could have just tripped on one of them.

For all we know that might be true.

Without me, you can do nothing . . .

She has no children. It's not an old folks' home. It was only a dream, that time he raped her with the pruning shears. It was only a dream that time they laughed as they drove along in his car.

I can't explain to you why she has to watch it, though, over and over and over again. Or what it is about Ewing, or that muddy mess of a ravine.

Hey, my life's no movie. Listen, I am very, very tired.

But he wanted me to tell him everything, and God, if I could, for him I would do it. He's become some kind of emblem of something for me, they all have. Something about tangled vines and worrisome blood cells, about tidy gravestones—more of them than you can count. How it seems necessary to do this because these boys I knew are dead—necessary, and also quite impossible.

Why "Sarah"? Obvious. It's biblical. The "h" is how you know that.

There's the problem of the stains on her clothing. There's the fact that she stumbles out of bed, drunk. There's the fact that she has no children. She is kicking up some fine, powdery dust in the garden. She just keeps on going back for more. What do you do with a woman like that? How do you make it all turn out, add up, reach a point, a juncture, a node?

Put her in that Trans Am, then. No more little yapping dog, no more David or Jerry or Mark or Rob. Just her behind the wheel, late for church, leaving the library or the shopping mall, a donut or a cookie in her hand, her fingers slippery with the sweet, sticky sugar of the thing.

Put the car on a narrow country road. Maybe now somewhere in Massachusetts, she's come that far east, on her own, let's say. Look through her eyes, through the windshield, at all she's seeing there.

No more straight lines. No more perfect tennis court grids. This road keeps *curving*; it's all she can do to keep from flying off its edge, despite that tug, that pull to some kind of center, somewhere, whatever it is that's pulling her on.

She isn't drunk.

She isn't all that old.

She's looking out the window and remembering some little side road somewhere, leading back to the old folks' home. When was she there? Was it here or someplace else?

She's still driving, maybe a bit too fast, one hand on the wheel, the other covered, remember, with that shiny, sticky sweetness.

She thinks she sees the road. Could that be it? Are my children down there? she wonders.

She keeps on looking, but probably she shouldn't do that. She isn't drunk, she's not that old, but she is very, very tired. The road she's on keeps branching, but she's looking for a certain one, a different one. There's something, though, that will not let her turn, some vine pulling this branching road back to some dark heartbeat center. She's going faster and faster, her right shoe that's worn at the left toe pushing the pedal farther and farther toward the floor. She keeps looking out to the side for something else. Maybe she shouldn't do that, maybe she should keep her eyes on the road because when she does look back, looks straight in front of her through the windshield, she realizes, too late, that very soon the road will curve sharply to the left, onto a narrow little bridge.

That's where the road goes. But what's in front of her, where she's driving, is water, some vast body of brown water, and she's going too fast now to ever make that curve. So that's where we'll leave her, where we will last see her. Though we can't really see her because we're there inside the thing, inside that silly teenage car, looking through her eyes and through the windshield at what's ahead. Which is water, just a great expanse of water. Brown and moving in waves, pulsing there like blood.

3. La Facultad

It is an acute awareness mediated by the part of the psyche that does not speak, that communicates in images and symbols which are the faces of feelings, that is, behind which feelings reside/hide. The one possessing this faculty is excruciatingly alive to the world. —Gloria Anzaldúa, *Borderlands: La Frontera*

At the Taos Pueblo our guide, Edward, explains to us how his people manage to blend the figures and faith of Spanish Catholicism with their own native religious traditions, and even though it's one of the clearest and loveliest explanations of this (to me) odd phenomenon, I've soon forgotten it. There is something that stands in the way of that kind of momentous simultaneity in my hopelessly Old World, black-and-white, good-and-evil mind. I have been trained to be rational. Still, there's something haunting about that clear, clear river flowing through the sleepy Pueblo (we've come early, before the later rush of cars and tourists) and also about Edward's achingly beautiful, long dark hair. From the vantage point of a little foot bridge, I watch an old dog lounge at the water's edge and feel, strangely enough, momentarily jealous.

Because as always I'm having trouble relaxing. I have, I'm convinced, a nagging Eastern tourist's brand of altitude sickness. Though lately, traveling anywhere always seems to leave me constipated and nursing a cold. But there is also this constant, just-below-the-surface headache, these perpetually stopped-up ears. I'm a basket case, and I hate my traveler self. In one of the little shops within the adobe walls the smell of burning piñon takes me out of my sorry, sniffling state for a moment, and I buy earrings and a little clay pot with the ubiquitous image of Kokopelli. Symbol of music and rain and fertility—all good things, I think (several weeks later my husband will knock it from a shelf and break it, and I will refuse to think too hard about this). In the church at the Taos Pueblo the small, life-like Virgin at the front (who looks strikingly like a doll I had when I was a child) is dressed in different colors for the different seasons. Now, in early spring, she has recently been changed from an Easter-white frock to a green one. In the cemetery, which is not particularly near the church, there is a wooden headstone with an inscription that begins, "Life and death are one, even as the river and sea are one." All of which is nice, I think, but I'm still constipated and more and more cars are arriving, making it considerably harder for me to ignore what I am: a tourist interloper with messed-up sinuses. I'm standing on a foot bridge over the hauntingly clear river, and Edward has begun another, bigger tour.

* * *

First I dream that my mother is standing at the foot of the bed, behind a cash register, while my husband and I make love. Then that I'm being played by Kim Novak in a movie and in the final scene, she/I am found hiding and crying behind a pile of boxes in the basement of my parents' home by William Holden, who takes her/me into his arms as the music swells. The next day we drive through the mountains to the towns of Las Trampas, Truchas, and finally, Chimayo, once, according to our guide book, the "place of banishment for serious offenders." Now Chimayo is noted for two things: its weaving and its 1814 adobe church, called Santuario del Señor de Esquipulas. Legend has it that the church's builder, Don Bernado Abeyta, was told in a vision to dig in the ground where the church is now built—and when he did he found a crucifix and was cured of a serious illness. Inside the Santuario the first thing I see looks like a tombstone, and it says "In memory of all the unborn victims of the crime of abortion," or something along those lines. No healing here, I think, almost on my way out the door, just another Catholic assault on women, not to mention my personal history and present preoccupation. But the sloping, shoe-smoothed floor and the folk art of the altar draw me in despite myself, and in a little room to the side (where twenty or more pairs of crutches hang from hooks on the wall, along with hundreds of pictures and notes from the healed, the cured, the miraculously pregnant) I go ahead and dip my fingers into Don Bernado Abeyta's famed hole of red, dusty dirt, hoping that at least my ears might clear. They don't, but as I walk back into the main sanctuary I do hear a clear and distinct and, for a church, unusual sound—a kind of merry war whoop. At the entrance I see two men and a woman supporting a boy, really a young man I see as I get closer; language gives way to sensitive feelings here, but in the past he would have been called a spastic. And he is yelling for joy in this beautiful room where everyone else is hushed. The priest emerges then and greets him warmly. "Here is my friend!" he says with relish to two women who are walking by with their heads bowed, and the priest and the spastic are noisy and joyful together. Later, I watch as his parents and older brother—all of them tall, lean, and serious, with Indian features, carrying such a weight—try gently to contain his flailing arms and ease him into the back seat of their car. And for a moment my ears, this mountain air, everything—all of it is devastatingly clear.

Echo Guilt

It's true, I think, that one of the more absurd habits of human consciousness is our tendency to be moved by animals that mate for life. And yet absurd or not, more than once I've found myself standing at my kitchen sink, weeping over two hummingbirds staying close together in my garden, flitting amongst the evening primroses whose opening, in the shadowy light of those heady summer evenings, I sometimes hardly noticed.

More often than not, on those evenings at the sink, I'd be washing dinner dishes for one—my own. I don't even know that it's true of hummingbirds, that they mate for life. It's possible I've made this up.

When did permanence become such a critical value? I could have tried to trace the history of this passion for things, for bonds, that endure. I could have tracked its development through one form of analysis or another—in the culture at large, in myself. But more often than not questions like these made me tired. On good nights, they would drive me to the garden. On good nights I'd recall that the dishes could wait, as could these questions. And I'd wonder how I'd managed to ignore the dusk-scented ritual of my primroses' nightly blooming for so long.

One day in the summer my husband, Jack, found a frog at the edge of our vegetable garden, in the back yard behind this house that we've rented, three hours north of New York City on a steep slope up from the Hudson River. Convinced that this was an animal that had somehow strayed too far from its native environment—surely the river—Jack teased the frog into a paper bag. Then, feeling that it was important to conserve time, he got in his jeep and drove the frog in the paper bag down to the park at the river's edge, two minutes away.

When he returned he said he felt ridiculous. When he got to the park there were a father and two children there, and suddenly Jack felt terribly embarrassed to have driven to the river's edge with a frog in a paper bag. But he was there and at that point it seemed there could be no going back, so he went ahead and opened the bag to let the frog go free.

"Such eco-guilt," he said, and shook his head at his own naïve earnestness. What if the frog *liked* it here, had no desire to be by the river, might even have to struggle to survive there, he suddenly wondered, and for a moment he looked worried.

I was sitting at the kitchen table, reading the paper, listening rather distractedly to him—something I often did, especially since he'd started selling more of his work, spending more and more time in the city and coming back full of stories that I somehow didn't want to hear.

When he said it, I thought he'd said "echo guilt" for some reason. "Such echo guilt." I nodded and made some sort of noise that said, "I know what you mean."

Because (A) three days before I'd killed all those baby spiders, an act that appalled me when I stopped, ten seconds into it, to catch my breath. (B) Two days before I'd been unable to make the drive into Albany for my weekly appointment with a therapist and lunch with a friend—my only contact with the outside world each week, really—because when I went out to get in my car there was what simply had to be a dead bird fetus on the hood, where it must have fallen from a tree branch above. And (C) the night before, when Jack came back from New York full of more stories and successes, I said things along these lines to him in my mind: "You've forgotten what you came here for. You're prostituting yourself. You're pandering to greedy, narcissistic New Yorkers who don't have a clue about what it is you see, and you're so flattered by big sales that before long you aren't going to remember what you used to see, either."

Some or all of which might have been true, but if I'd actually said it all aloud we both would've known why, and where all my bitterness came from. We wouldn't have had to say a word.

And so on. And D, E, F, G, and on and on, growing farther away and fainter, but still there.

Here's something interesting about living in a place like this: On the little country roads around our house, no one immediately whisks the road-kill away the way they obviously do on major highways (though you never see them do it, which seems odd). So you can drive home over the course of a week or so and see a dead animal going through various stages of decomposition, until it's no longer recognizable. One Labor Day weekend, however, even the New York State Thruway fell behind on the magical clean-up. Driving south toward the city was like navigating an asphalt sea clogged with dead animals. All gray squirrels.

Later I learned that that fall was a migratory one for gray squirrels, a cyclical thing that happens every five to ten years or so. Gray squirrels could never have anticipated the rise of the U.S. interstate highways. When they need to move west, or south, or wherever, how could they possibly avoid those relentless roads?

So some make it, and some don't. And we steer around the dead ones as best we can, clutching the wheel and gritting our teeth and hoping that the next migrating squirrel doesn't choose to make its desperate dash in front of our own car's tires.

Something about that reminded me of urban dwellers' convoluted efforts—when walking, driving, taking buses—to avoid poor neighborhoods. Funny, but people at our upstate grocery store use food stamps, too. And nobody clears the dead animals from the country roads. So nice try, I tell myself, if it's guilt you're trying to get away from.

I left what's called a "good job"—a writing job, of sorts—to do this, to live somewhere else, far away from the trials of city living. In what I *should* think of as an incredible stroke of luck, I know I should, just at the time I quit my job Jack got a gallery show and started bringing in a semi-comfortable income from his photographs.

This meant we could move, we could finally get the space, the air we'd always wanted, get away from the city. And, as Jack kept reminding me, I could write the things I wanted to write, never mind what anyone else said.

I could be researching things like the emphasis we all seem to place on permanence. I could be writing things I like to write. But the truth is, since we left the city, I've barely written a thing.

Instead, I garden. When Jack left for the city again the day after the frog incident, I went out to weed the tomatoes, secretly hoping that the frog might be back, making a complete wash of Jack's good deed. Jack has done too many good deeds. And I haven't done enough. Birds die on my car, I kill spiders. And me writing? It feels like a distant memory, a tune I can barely hear.

But at the height of summer, tiny white alyssum blossoms tumble out of wood flower boxes on our back porch, and there are thick leaves of basil at the edge of the vegetable garden. I don't know how to do this, I'm making it up as I go. When something dies—even just a spindly pot of nasturtiums outside the too-shaded front door—I feel like I've committed some kind of crime. When it suddenly turned bitterly cold and snowed in April after an unusually warm March, I went to bed in a profound depression, fearing for the budding trees.

It sounds almost comical, but when it's happening it's not. When I worked in the back yard that first summer, I avoided the third wood flower box on the porch, the one the mother spider lived under. If I saw her, I knew it, I'd have to go inside for a long time. It's good Jack was home so little in those days; if he saw what really went on, I'm not sure what he would have thought.

Not too long after we moved into this rented house, we drove by a remarkable stone farmhouse—seventeenth century, in fact, speaking of permanence. It had a For Sale sign, and in what we decided to think of as a completely uncharacteristic gesture, for us (artist Jenny Holzer's "Private Property Is a Crime" message swirled by on an electronic signboard in my mind), we called the realtor and set up an appointment.

It definitely needed some work. And the price could have been terribly high or terribly low; it made little difference really, considering we were starting from nothing (both financially and, at that point, emotionally). Driving away we were silent for a while, then nervously laughing. What were we thinking? Just kind of fun, right? To imagine that for just a moment. Kind of a lark. A distraction.

At the time, we were not yet married. In fact, Jack was thinking seriously, then, of returning to the city. Things between us were that strained.

It seems so long ago, that first visit to the stone house. I've lost all sense of the season, though I seem to recall that it was cold. Living here, gardening, seeing things die (in the fall my cats carry in chipmunks, which usually live, and birds, which usually don't), I have confused seasonal memories. In the dead of winter I envision the spot, buried under snow, where my lawn chair rests each late summer afternoon. In the sticky heat of summer I find myself imagining white, a snow-cold purity, an alyssum bed of the mind.

In New York there was basically heavy-coat, jacket, and shorts weather. But now, here, it seems that the more distinct the seasons are, the more they jumble up and cross circuits in my brain. I do know, though, that the next time we drove by the old stone farmhouse, it was a blustery, gray Easter Sunday—springtime in upstate New York. We had decided to get married, the For Sale sign was gone, and all the windows were boarded shut. I felt like someone had punched me in the stomach.

Why should Jack's success seem to stifle me so? And why should I worry so about that previous summer's rash return to some kind of childish fear, that mindless, terrorized batting with the broom when I realized that the shiny spots on the webs crisscrossing the flower box were not dewdrops but spider eggs? And that the more I batted, the more tiny spiders, already born, scattered in a thousand directions. Why wonder, later, in the midst of a snowstorm, where the mother spider has gone?

Feeding stray cats is some solace. Their matted fur and hostile hisses seem right. I'd resent my feeble charity, too. The hand that feeds you can just as easily kill you. Always stay alert.

A friend has sent gladiola bulbs. So far I've resisted most of the gardening coffee table books, *Gardening* magazine, the various wintertime catalogs. I don't know how to plant gladiola bulbs, however. When? Where? Inside, blank white sheets of paper, blank white computer screen. Outside, a blank sheet of white, white snow.

But a brown bird sits at the feeder, crunching black seed. Time passes.

We are married, and it never stops snowing. Jack is not impressed by winter in the country this year. Orders, invitations are slowing down. We haven't driven by the stone farmhouse in a while. Picturing it in this relentless winter wash, I'm glad for the boards on the windows. But intrigued, too—and a little frightened—by the thought of something trapped inside.

The problem with the gardening books and magazines is that they make it all look too beautiful. The dirt looks *clean*; there are no earthworms, no rotting compost. No death. Don't be fooled—too much neatness is a curse, in gardens and elsewhere.

My problem may be that I would like there to be a precise equation. Some kind of animal kingdom logic. Why do we treat one another badly? The couple who owned the stone house had great plans for its renovation. Then their youngest child graduates from high school, the husband meets a younger woman, and so on. An old story about what comes after the fairy-tale wedding part. So the wife is left to try to sell the house.

I don't know where she is now. But I imagine her boarded-up house through the various seasons, slowly sinking into the ground. Hewn stone's gradual return to the earth. An American ruin. Younger than in Greece or Rome, but we all know that rock is rock.

I think of Virginia Woolf, of her "Time Passes" section in the middle of *To the Lighthouse*. The Ramsays' abandoned house slowly succumbing to the ravages of time—books molding, birds nesting, gardens fiercely overgrown. From here I move (and are literature and suicide adequate reasons for this connection, I wonder?) to Sylvia Plath. Caught in her crawlspace, father's boot at her neck. Thinking she might be a Jew. I'm not sure what I think of her thinking this. But I do know that more and more I feel afraid of the neatness-obsessed Nazi in all of us. Jack feels stymied these days, but his work table is immaculate. I close the newspaper on a picture of a starved orphan girl in China and turn to the business of organizing my recipes. Even though I'm not the least bit hungry.

There's an unlimited catalog of cruelties, great and small, out there. In here too, if you care to look. And it all gets handed down. Diluted maybe, fainter, but still there.

My seven-year-old nephew, I'm told, watched a documentary about Hiroshima on television and afterwards sobbed, inconsolable. At times like that you want words that will take flight with him on board, candles floating on water, the lovely certainty and sanctity of a Japanese garden. But really, what can you say—that they didn't mean it?

We understand pain and cruelty far better at seven than at thirty-seven. I know that in that clear and tear-choked state my nephew enters sometimes he would simply say, They always mean it. And he would be right.

Brown bird in winter, faded romance, boarded windows, buried stone.

I wish I could take back so many things. Thought, said, done. Echo guilt. We live with such certainty, and sometimes you have to wonder why.

But of course it's true that spring will come, and white will change to gray, then brown, then green. The boards will come off the windows. Light and dust will return. The sound of the wind, birds seeking homes. Crocus leaves will force their way through soil that's barely thawed.

And, most miraculous of all perhaps, some mates will remain mates. Two still together. For no apparent reason, licking at nectar next to each other, staying close but tentative, suspended by wings that bat a silent breeze. Despite those years of doubts and fears and vicious, vicious crimes.

Fallow

In the woods around her the invisible cricket choruses had struck up, but what she heard were the voices of the souls climbing upward into the starry field and shouting hallelujah.

—Flannery O'Connor, "Revelation"

When the wind blew through the dry, papery leaves of the woods behind the high school, a chorus of cicadas joined the rising, swelling wave of late-summer sound. Anne Louise Bowman held her breath, let her chest cave in with the weight until the wave subsided, rolled back, a moment's reprieve before the next round of hot, dry wind and singing insects.

She breathed out into the silence. Later, surely, there would be a storm—rain at last, release.

She smiled at the image of a wave, here in this flat valley, this landlocked midwestern prairie worlds away from any ocean or sea. She stared out the window of her empty classroom at the burnt brown grass. When the cicadas trilled again, it was as if each blade of grass had somehow found a voice and cried out in the agony of this three o'clock August heat.

She had just finished rereading Flannery O'Connor's "Revelation." Her pulse beat faster and faster, as it always did, as she read up to the critical moment, the letting loose, the flying free of a clenched spring—when ugly, acne-ridden Mary Grace from

Wellesley College lets fly the Human Development book, striking Mrs. Turpin square above her left eye. And then, her fateful, clear-eyed whisper: "Go back to hell where you came from, you old wart hog."

Anne Louise imagined saying this to Barbara Stevens, the typing teacher, who did in fact resemble a wart hog and whose smug, self-righteous image she always drew on when she pictured Mrs. Turpin. Or better yet, from the back row of the band room, at the dreadful beginning-of-the-year faculty meeting, slamming shut her Harbrace English Handbook and throwing it with might and finesse, watching it curve in a graceful arc above the rows of impassive music stands and bland backs of teachers' heads, before connecting, perfectly, with the principal Mr. Hodges' shiny left temple. Just to the inside of his dark brown sideburn, which, when seen in profile, looked disturbingly like the left sideburn of her husband, John.

John was a principal, too, but at a different school—a larger one in a wealthier town, twenty miles away. He was a coach as well—esteemed, beloved, at home in his world in a way Anne Louise knew she would never be.

The cicadas sang out in loud, ascending unison. Just when she thought the sound might make her cry or make her mad, it died away again.

Every year at this time, she read "Revelation" again and toyed, briefly, momentarily intoxicated by the notion, with the idea of assigning the story to her twelfth-grade students. And this year, as every year before, her initial excitement faded as she imagined the reactions of these students—children, all of them, of parents who were perfect clones of Claud and Ruby Turpin, the hog-farming couple at the center of O'Connor's story.

That is to say—the wind swelled and her heart and stomach sank as she thought of it—they wouldn't understand, they'd see no reason to react at all when Ruby Turpin wonders to herself what, if Jesus forced her to pick, she would choose to be: a nigger or white trash.

They would have an intuitive sense of what was meant by "white trash," some of them. Except for the ones who belonged, undeniably, in that category themselves. "Nigger" would make some of them giggle, others squirm in their seats.

Someone would complain to Mr. Hodges, who would object, in his usual ignorance, to the use of such labels. If he bothered to read the story at all, if he even grasped any of it, he would find it troubling in its ambiguity about spiritual matters.

That would be his assessment of Flannery O'Connor. Troubling. And therefore bad.

The truth was, the story seemed to her to reach its climax there in the middle, in the scene in the doctor's waiting room, when Mary Grace bursts furiously into Ruby Turpin's narrow-minded, hog-filled world. The truth was, as far as Anne Louise was concerned, the story could have ended there. She knew the real "revelation" was supposed to come at the end, with Ruby Turpin's strange vision, of pigs and hogs and niggers and white trash and people like herself, all together at last, all ascending the long stairs up to heaven. And she knew that if she ever actually assigned the story, she'd have to deal with that oddly uplifting image at the end.

But that was just Flannery O'Connor's Catholicism getting in the way of a good story, as far as Anne Louise was concerned. For her, the most glorious moment came square in the middle, with that leveling blow to the old hypocrite's temple, and the hissing, whispered advice to her to go back to hell where she came from.

A broom brushed by her open door, reminding her of the hour. The custodians were cleaning, though there wasn't yet any noticeable dirt, sweeping the air in the empty halls. The other teachers would be gone by now, football practice starting up. Classes were to start the next week, the first football game was set for that Friday, and there wasn't even a hint, not the slightest smell, of fall in the air.

The ground and the leaves were the burnt brown-yellow of late summer. Their color made her dizzy, and a little nauseated. John would expect dinner promptly at six o'clock, even though she'd gone back to work as well. But there should be time enough for cooking, as they didn't have a child. As that had not happened, and would not happen now. As some part of her, something deep within her, would keep her womb an arid plain as visible to her mind's eye as the brown grass outside her classroom window.

In the end, Mrs. Turpin saw the souls of pigs and hogs climbing the long, steep stairs to heaven. Pigs and hogs, "a-gruntin and a-rootin and a-groanin," in the words of the white trash girl in the waiting room, the one who thanked "Gawd" she wasn't a pig. Or a nigger.

Anne Louise searched in her bag for her car keys before stepping out into the blinding afternoon. In the parking lot the sun beat down on the hot new asphalt; it looked soft enough to sink in, and it smelled strongly of oil. The bright yellow lines that marked the empty spaces stung her tired eyes, causing her to squint.

The lines were new this year. Last spring, on the last day of school for the seniors, Mike Eckard—one of her favorite students because of his unfailing irreverence—had led a handful of other seniors in a small rebellion. They parked their cars every which way in the parking lot—some backwards, some at odd angles. Mike's pick-up truck was parked sideways, square in the middle of the front row, which was reserved for teachers. In its back window was a large white posterboard with the message, "You give us no lines, no direction. How are we supposed to know where we should be?"

There was a tense stand-off between Mike and Mr. Hodges the whole morning, delaying the annual honors assembly for two hours, until finally, at ten-thirty, Mike and the others put their cars back in neat, tidy rows at the back of the lot, all pointing respectfully toward the school. It might have gone on longer if several of the young rebels hadn't had to get to their one o'clock shifts at the paper mill that afternoon.

The teachers, of course, were expected to maintain a grave, tight-lipped countenance in response to the "crisis," saying nothing. And Anne Louise had complied, except for a brief, appreciative chuckle—that roused an angry glare from Barbara Stevens—with her friend Susan, who taught health and human development, in the teachers' lounge earlier that morning. But later, at the honors assembly, she made a point of catching Mike's eye as he passed her row during the seniors' procession and giving him a small, approving nod.

Now Mike worked in a factory on the edge of the town where John was the happy high school principal. Mike's young wife was pregnant. This, of course, was why she was his wife instead of his girlfriend, which would make more sense for two people as young as they were, as Anne Louise knew. Mike couldn't afford college on his own, and his parents could see no reason for him to go. The guidance counselor decided his high test scores didn't mean much when you considered what a bad attitude he had.

"How are we supposed to know where we should be?"

"A-gruntin and a-rootin and a-groanin . . ."

Driving home, Anne Louise drove over the little bridge above Sugar Creek, normally a wide, circling stream with tiny waterfalls shining brilliant in the sun, but now, in this unforgiving August heat, a dry bed of cracked gray mud. As she had that morning on her way in to school, she pulled over to the side of the road and walked down to the edge of the creek bed, below the bridge.

She looked for what she'd left there that morning—a little pool of vomit in the shadow of the bridge—and found it soon enough. The midday sun had reached it, drying it, making it nearly indistinguishable from the powdery mud it lay in, save for the little flecks of yellow egg, angry vestiges of the breakfast her body had refused.

There was no shade, no relief anywhere, and she stood there in the pounding sun until she felt as if she were swimming, circling in waves of a thick liquid heat. The cicadas were screaming furiously, directly into her ear; their voices rose and rose, never falling, never pausing for breath. She thought that they might leave her deaf.

At last she drove home without the air conditioner, soaking quietly, unmoving, in a sheath of her own sweat. Home, where she would wait, quiet and still, for the rain that she knew would never come.

Fitness Tests

Sometimes they walked in the woods.

Then she would step gingerly over the layers of leaves rich with the sweet smell of their own rotting. Below them, she knew, were hidden patches of wet brown mud; she would make a mental note to take a tissue from her purse and wipe the low heels of her shoes before going back to work.

They didn't walk there often because of the risk. Usually they sat in a dimly lit bar with a Polynesian theme, seashell patterns on a velvet background above their heads. The window beside them was safely blocked by faded, heavy curtains that smelled of a smoky, disappointed past.

She'd stare at the gold band below his swollen knuckle, all his fingers fat with success. She'd twist her own in endless circles as she listened.

Sometimes she barely had time to eat, he had so much to say.

Then they'd get in their cars and drive the ten miles back to their town, to their jobs, his at his own law office, hers at the bank.

When she drove past the high school she checked the parking lot for her son's car and each time, when she saw it, she felt she could breathe normally at last, felt she could relax then, felt normal again, without knowing what that meant.

Her husband's hands and feet are ice against her skin at night. She feels herself suffocating, gasping for air beneath his merciless weight.

Deeper in the night, she knows, she is grinding her teeth. In the morning her jaw aches, and her teeth are tender when she grazes them with her tongue.

She doesn't want to see the dentist. There is the expense, and the questions he would ask might overwhelm her, she thinks.

When they were first married her husband would lie awake at night and listen to the noise of the grinding. It was almost like metal, he said, the harsh scraping of the enamel, almost like something he would hear at his job. He stroked her shoulder while she slept, her jaw clenched, a war waging inside her.

In the morning he would tell her, "You did it again last night." Then, "You stopped after I rubbed your shoulder for a while." She would thank him then, as expected, clearing the breakfast table in a rush.

She saw the only dentist in town at the time, the one she'd seen since she was a child.

"It's hard at first to be married," he had said as he patted her shoulder.

At lunch or when they walked together in the woods, he told her his problems. About the daughter, in her second year at the State University, how he couldn't understand her and couldn't stand her friends.

How young and inexperienced the other men in his office were. How cold and silent his wife had become.

When she drove by the high school parking lot and saw her son's car there, she told herself it was all right as long as he didn't touch her. The most he had done was to place a hand at the small of her back, quickly and discreetly, guiding her from the parking lot to the entrance to the bar. That small touch alone had made her arch her back, clench each muscle in readiness, she didn't know for what. And after that, he hadn't tried to guide her again.

As long as it went no further than that, though, no further than an occasional pat or a guiding arm, she felt it would be fine.

Once they tried the woods in the State Park in November, at the early edges of winter. But it was too cold to walk outside so they sat in his car with the engine idling softly. She'd been afraid then, unsure of what it might mean, to him, for her to sit there with him in his car.

But before long another car pulled in at the entrance and he quickly backed the car out of his spot and drove out of the parking area. She turned her head, her hand at her neck, as the two cars passed, but in the rear-view mirror she saw it was a car she recognized, the rusted-out Trans Am of one of her son's friends.

When her son was a boy she would leave the bank at five minutes to three and drive to the school to pick him up. They'd stop at the grocery store and then drive home and he would tell her all about his day.

Now he comes home late, smelling of cigarettes and beer. He eats his dinner in silence, barely telling her hello. She has no idea how to reach him. Sometimes she feels sure that he knows everything, everything there is to know about her.

She has dreams of drowning, the same dreams she had when she was a girl, of foundering in a deep, cold river, coughing and sputtering as the water fills her lungs, fighting but sinking, thinking it would never be over, that she would never breathe normally again.

One morning she wakes from the dream in a cold sweat, her jaw throbbing, the blankets in wild disorder at her feet.

She looks over at her husband, snoring senselessly on his side, his white skin glowing pale in the cold, moonlit air of their bedroom.

In her dream the pool was a giant blue expanse under a curved and ancient dome, all of it covered with flaking ivory tiles. Her husband stood alone at the pool's edge, a young man, really just a boy—the way he'd been when they were first married —standing in his baggy swim trunks, shivering in the cold.

She thinks of the story he told her about the first and only year he went to college, in the days when all the men at the State University had to pass various physical fitness tests, including one in swimming. Like her, like all the farm kids they knew growing up, he'd never learned to swim. So he did the ten laps by flailing wildly in the water, gasping desperately for air, feeling, truly, that he might die from the exhaustion and the shame.

When he finished the others were long gone. Only the physical education instructor in his crisp, white pants and sneakers remained, standing at the edge of the pool with his clipboard, checking off her husband's name with obvious contempt.

He decided, after that first year, that college wasn't for him. He came back to their home town then, working first in the cement plant and then, when the back-breaking labor and the fine, powdery dust that was slowly accumulating in his lungs got to be too much, moving over to the lumberyard where he worked now.

She lies there in the quiet night, her joints stiff and aching, her breathing, it seems to her, unbearably labored and loud in that stillness, unable to shake the image of her husband's pale, skinny legs below his swimming trunks, hairless and nearly blue with the cold.

At last she shudders and then she sighs. She pulls the blankets back over her, turning onto her side, turning her tired and weakened back to his own.

What Alma Knows

This year at Christmas Alma's nephew Richard has a new van and this means she has a single seat entirely to herself, no children kicking at her knees and less reason for senseless chatter with Richard's wife, Jean. So Alma is staring out at the landscape, which, like most years, is decidedly flat and brown.

Now and then they roll over a hill and the terrain could almost be called pretty but there will always be a row of ugly little matchbox houses there to ruin it, Alma knows. Alma knows that in her youth it all looked different—there weren't those horrible little houses for one thing—and she thinks there must have been more snow then, too. Winter must have been white in those days but now each year as they drive to the family Christmas party at her niece's outside Bloomington it is always just this same gray shade of brown.

Alma's grandniece, Janet, is eighteen and she isn't saying much either, and Alma believes she might know why. Janet's furrowed brow is like a cloud drooping over her angry eyes, reining in the weather, the storm that's brewing there.

Alma tries not to stare too obviously, because at just that moment a different image of her niece is forming in her mind—smiling, laughing, seated on the floor in a dim or smoky room while someone's fingers stroke her long blonde hair. The image seems to vibrate at the corner of Alma's brain but the moment she grasps it fully it's suddenly gone, vanished into the stuffy air of the van, and Janet is, once again, seated there across from her, silent and withdrawn.

Alma considers asking Richard to turn down the heat but decides against it. This year the long, boring drive in the hot and airless van is bothering her less than other years. This year she's got what she's done to the divinity to think about.

"Glad we're not driving to Chicago!" Richard roars from the front seat, as he's done each year for a while now at just this point in the drive. It's the mileage sign that reminds him, Alma knows.

Jean laughs and rolls her eyes, and her words are wrapped inside a soft and quiet whistle when she says, "Me too." The twins, who are ten, look up for a moment from their computer games to smile and nod, and as they do Alma, stunned by their size, by how they've grown, realizes they wouldn't be kicking her knees at all now. They wouldn't have kicked her knees for years in fact—riding there in the back seat with her, crawling back and forth between her lap and that of their mother—and Alma is frightened for a moment as she wonders where the years in between went, what corner of her unreliable brain they might have escaped to at that moment.

Janet says nothing about the year they all drove to their cousin John's in the Chicago suburbs, the first and last time they held the party there, when Richard, confused by the countless lanes and signs on the interstate and overwhelmed by the traffic, got them hopelessly lost and well into Wisconsin before he realized it. When Janet, who was twelve then, asked in total innocence (or was it?, Alma has always wondered) if it mattered that they were no longer in Illinois, Richard snapped at her, "God damn it, Janet, of course it matters! Do you think I'm happy about this, d'you think I wanted to have this goddamn party in Chicago to begin with?" with a level of fury that took them all by surprise.

They were two hours late that year, and they left early because it had started to snow and Richard was worried about the roads. Janet spent the entire brief time they were there in an upstairs bedroom, until her father went to talk to her and she appeared, her face red and splotchy, to open her gifts.

Now, Alma sees it coming and she wishes she could stop it but she has no idea how. She knows it's absurd and she knows he has to do it, that there's something almost forcing him to do it. He's his father's son, her brother's son, and they all spring from her father, the true master of this particular brand of quiet cruelty that Richard reserves for his teenage daughter.

"Remember that year, Jan?" he asks, grinning back at his daughter, who sits slumped in the seat across from Alma. Janet's head leans against the cold window—and as Alma stares at her she feels a blast of cold from the window at her own left side—and she is tracing endless circles in the steam left by her own breath.

Janet says nothing, only glances at her father and shrugs. Alma clears her throat into the uncomfortable silence and glances at the silk scarf she holds on her lap.

The scarf was a gift last year, from Jean and Richard. They have been good to her, Alma thinks, and despite herself she finds she wants to cry. Richard mows the front lawn, which is more than she can handle; though the housing developments on the edge of town are gradually eating up all that's left of the farm, the lawn is still quite large. And when she slipped on the ice and broke her hip three years before, Jean visited her every day in the hospital and looked in on the house and took in her mail.

Richard is the youngest son of Alma's brother, who died ten years before. He is the only one who's stayed on there in the town and of course that means it has fallen to him to look after her. The spinster aunt. Every family needs a spinster aunt, she thinks to herself, and she tries to decide whether he's resented it. He's never shown any outward signs, but after he finishes mowing he always stays outside to drink the glass of lemonade she offers him, standing at the edge of the porch and staring out at the new houses going up in the distance.

One day it will be his, the house and what's left of the land. God only knows what he'll do with it, Alma thinks. She's stopped caring, really, what he does. She tells herself it doesn't matter now that her father and her brother, the only ones who'd ever loved the house and farm to begin with, are dead.

They all feel sorry for her that she never married, she knows, but when she thinks of her father and mother, of her brother, of Richard and Jean, she can't think that it would have been any better. Perhaps she might have married Wesley Miller, but when she thinks of him she thinks only of dry, brown grass and a creaking of bones, a strange and frightening creaking of bones that she knows she heard but seemed somehow not to feel, and dry, brown grass like straw and late sun in the afternoon. When he took her hand and led her and her father didn't tell her not to go and her mother was in the kitchen baking, always baking. Now in the overheated car the memory makes her shudder.

And Wesley Miller would not have married her. That she knows. Not after that. But never mind, she tells herself. It's water under the bridge, and about marriage never mind.

Alma's hands move from the warm silk of her scarf to the cold metal of the cookie tin she holds on her lap and the cold, round rim in her hand is comforting.

It isn't that they aren't all good to her, but every year they grow fatter and more smug, and every year she knows that she is thinner, her bones closer than ever to the cold white surface of her skin, and as she grows older and thinner there seems to be less and less of her there, less of her to occupy a space in her niece Linda's pale blue living room with the artificial Christmas tree decked out all in white. White balls, white lights, and that was all. And each year Alma feels as light and inconsequential as one of those white balls made of cheap silk threads, ready to blow away, ready to curl and melt into nothing from the heat of those white lights.

Last year, when everyone gathered their serving platters, their empty bowls of stuffing or noodles or mashed potatoes, Alma went to gather her candy tin and discovered that not one piece of the divinity she made had been eaten. She saw that Linda, who was standing right beside her licking jello from her fingers, had noticed, too, and Alma's cheeks burned with shame.

Alma makes the divinity every year. The recipe was her mother's, and when she was a child—when snow still fell, when winter was not endlessly brown, when they didn't eat packaged desserts and no one's Christmas tree was done all in white, only white—her mother's divinity was Alma's favorite Christmas treat of all.

It isn't hard to make but it is hard to make well. She has to do it the day before and she has to heat the sugar and corn syrup and water to just the right temperature and she has to beat the egg whites until she is weak with exhaustion. She shapes little, lily-white dollops of sugar that are light as air—makes each one as perfectly neat and round as the one before (if it isn't she throws it out) and in the center of each she positions one small brown nut, one uniform pecan.

She always makes divinity at Christmas. When she was a young woman, before her mother died, they made it together. Never mind that over the last few years no one has seemed to want it much. Never mind that they would rather have chocolate chip cookies bought in a package, or plastic-wrapped candy in a box. She never makes it for herself—she no longer likes sweets, can't really stomach much of anything at these family dinners at Christmas. It's simply what she's always done, and what her mother did before her.

Alma beats the egg whites in an aged wooden bowl that was her mother's. She stopped oiling it long ago, and its edges have begun to crack.

When he took her hand and led her and the grass was brown and hot, her mother was baking bread. Bread, it had to be bread she was baking then.

She hadn't confessed. She did not tell the priest at confession but when she took communion, when the priest placed the host, milky white and light as air, at the center of her tongue, she choked. She choked and choked, coughing uncontrollably, and she had to leave the mass. But she never did confess, she never told the priest how her father said nothing and her mother went on baking and he took her hand, she let him take her hand, how in fact she did not tell him no.

This year, as she rubbed her chapped fingers over the cracked edges of her mother's wooden bowl, Alma heard the deafening silence in her kitchen, in her entire house. And something about that silence made her reach for the bottle of white vinegar on the top shelf of the pantry. The bottle, when she grasped it, seemed to vibrate in her hand.

This year Alma has altered her mother's divinity recipe. Instead of mixing a half cup of water with the sugar and the corn syrup she has used vinegar. There's the slightest vinegary smell to the little white clouds this year, faint and distant, a reminder of something gone sour. She grips the tin tightly as Richard turns off the highway onto one of the winding streets of the subdivision where his sister Linda lives. For a second she feels the buzzing again—hears breathless laughter, sees fingers stroking hair. But then Richard shuts off the engine and then he's opening her door, and the cold air feels like a punishing smack across her face.

When she enters Linda's pale blue house, Alma has the urge she has every year, to walk back out into the cold air, back to the safety of the car. Everyone greets her but without a great deal of warmth; she knows they don't know what to say to her, how to approach the spinster aunt.

Behind her she feels Linda's long, pointy fingernails reaching for her coat and hears her ask, "How've you been?"

"Fine" is all Alma says as she tucks her scarf into the sleeve of her coat, and that is all she says because she knows that that's all Linda wants to hear.

At the dinner table Alma is seated, as always, next to Linda's mother-in-law, the other lone old woman at the family Christmas gathering. And as they've done every year for longer than Alma can remember now, they exchange pleasantries and talk briefly about the weather and then eat the rest of their meal in silence, taking in bits and pieces of other conversations around them now and then, saying nothing. Linda's mother-in-law is eighty-eight, ten years older than Alma, and she seems ancient and tired. When Alma sits beside her, when she is told that this is her place, Alma feels older than all the rest of them put together.

Across the table Alma catches sight of Janet, who has only some salad and a few noodles that she's hardly touching on her plate. She's not talking to anyone, either, and her eyes, so dark and shadowed, dart from side to side at odd, unpredictable moments. Alma remembers feeling that way when she was a girl, remembers feeling, from time to time, that all eyes were on her and she'd better look up to meet those eyes dead on, lest she be stared at unawares, stared at without staring back.

She feels immense relief to know that now, at last, no one is ever looking. No one stares at her bony gray frame at all; she's free to look where she pleases, no more darting of anxious eyes for her.

Jean has talked to her, from time to time, about the problems they've had with Janet. About how she is so quiet and sullen, angry at them all the time, how she won't go out even in the summer, staying in her room instead, alone, reading books and listening to records. They tried taking Janet to a counselor of some kind, a psychologist, last year. They were worried about her going off to college this year with that kind of attitude. But Janet had nothing to say to the counselor, either.

Apparently she has made some friends at college. She brought one girl home at Thanksgiving, and Alma felt almost sorry she'd turned down Richard and Jean's invitation to join them for dinner when she heard about the girl. She called herself "Moon," Jean said, and one side of her head was shaved close to her scalp and the rest of her hair was tied in a lopsided ponytail. She had four earrings in one ear and five in the other, and sometimes when she and Janet went out to the mall in the evenings she wore what looked like a dog collar around her neck.

She never stopped talking at meals, Jean said. She asked them all kinds of questions, nosy ones really, about the family, about their neighbors and what not. It made Richard nervous—he'd always have to leave the table before dessert. And Richard swore that once he saw Moon stroking Janet's hair in the back seat of the car, when they thought no one was looking. But Jean said at least it was nice to see Janet smile at the dinner table for a change. Because apparently that's what she did, just sat there quietly and smiled at her friend Moon the whole time.

But Moon didn't come for Christmas and Janet isn't smiling now. Her father has made a couple of attempts to get her to talk about college, about her dorm and her classes and so forth during the course of the meal. But she has repeatedly answered him in one word ("Fine"—like Alma's response to Linda, she realizes), and Richard has finally given up, making no attempt to hide his frustration.

Alma knows Janet sees her silence as her one and only defense, the one way she has to defeat her father. But it's a victory that's hard to savor, Alma knows. Better to smile and laugh with the exotic Moon, she thinks—better that than a silence no one understands.

Alma would like to say this to her grandniece but she feels frightened of Janet somehow. When they stand to clear the table she catches the girl's eye and smiles at her, and she is pleased when Janet smiles back. Suddenly she gets a picture of herself with a half-shaved head and a dog collar around her neck, and she laughs quietly to herself as she opens her tin of divinity and places each piece carefully on a plate in Linda's kitchen. There's only a trace of the scent of vinegar on her fingertips as she places the plate on the dessert table, between an apple pie and something with chocolate pudding and whipped cream.

Later, she's sitting in a rocker next to Linda's mother-in-law—in the old women's corner again, and this time she's picked it herself—sipping her coffee and watching people file by the desserts. So far everyone has passed the divinity by, opting instead for the thicker, heavier things.

No one is talking to her and a chorus of words is gradually taking shape, growing louder, inside Alma's tired brain. Lonely old maid, she is thinking over and over, louder and louder. Lonely old maid in the corner in her rocker. Lonely old maid. Only lone maid.

And the words are there in countless voices, more than she can recognize, but at the bottom of them all there is one constant, buzzing bass voice; it's always there at the bottom, holding the line and insisting on a slow, relentless rhythm, and though Alma doesn't quite know this, what that buzzing is is the low, gravelly voice of her father. Only lone maid, it repeats. My only lone maid. Lemonade. Make me my lemonade, only lone maid, lonely old maid. Over and over he repeats it, and now the buzzing has grown so loud it's drowning out all other sound.

She'd made lemonade and they drank it on the porch, the glass cool and wet in her hand, her fingers still stinging from the sour, biting juice of the lemons. And he took her hand and led her—all the time her father saying nothing, sitting still and looking, saying nothing. Oh never mind, never mind. It was all just brown, brown grass and the flat, endless land. Sour lemonade and brown grass in the sun and the creaking bones, the brittle, creaking bones and the groan of muscle, breathless groan of muscle. Creaking bones and groaning muscle. And had she said yes? She hadn't said no, never mind, she hadn't said no. And the groaning, the strange, silent groaning inside. Groaning old maid, lone maid. Never mind, never mind.

The room seems foggy to her now. She is floating in the foggy blue room and now Janet is there, she is there at the dessert table, looking over to see Alma looking at her. Their eyes lock and Alma doesn't know how long it is before she sees that Janet's hand is reaching, slowly reaching, moving through the room's blue fog toward Alma's plate of sour white divinity. Alma sees an arm in a filmy white robe lifting out of the fog, lifting the bitter white host toward Janet's waiting mouth, its slow, searing acid about to burn into her waiting tongue.

And Alma is up then, springing up from her chair like a young woman, a young maid. She swims briskly through that fog and then she is there at Janet's side, standing there beside her angry, silent niece. The piece of white divinity is there in the girl's hand but she pauses as her great-aunt whispers in her ear.

What Alma says to her is, Don't. Simply that. Don't, Janet. Don't eat the divinity.

What she thinks, without quite knowing it, is, Wait instead. Wait for something different, something light as air but not so bitter on the tongue—wait, she thinks, for a white hot summer moon.

Stories about Miranda

"Let's talk about Miranda." Or, "Tell me about Miranda." Nine out of ten times he talked to me, the Birdman must've started out with a line like that.

They'd put me on the adolescent ward the second time I got sent to Jefferson State Hospital, thanks to the Birdman. He was the new man in charge, and he'd changed the whole thing around since my last nightmare stay there on the banks of the Ohio River, years before. It's true that I was over twenty, which in most people's eyes means older than adolescent, but I believe the Birdman would've said something like it was more a state of mind. Adolescence, I mean.

Looking back, I expect he'd say I was kinda stuck at around twelve or thirteen and that's what I was doin' there in the first place. But at the time, I didn't think so much about where they'd put me (I felt right at home there, so why think about it?). I was more interested in trying to figure out some kind of connection between two things. The first one was all the Birdman's questions about my mother, Miranda. The second one was the fact that I was there in that goddamn state hospital one more time because everyone in my home town of West Vernon, Indiana, had the idea that my favorite pastime was knocking on women's doors and then, when they answered, giving them their own private peep show right there on the front stoop.

I figured if I could just make out this connection the Birdman always seemed to be looking for, I could tell him what he wanted to hear and get on out of there. Not that I was in that big a rush. Before too long that second time, I realized I kinda liked it there. It was a world away from the piss-smelling hallways and army-booted orderlies on the ward they'd put me on when I was sixteen, I'll tell you that much. Put it this way: when I was the right age to be on one, there wasn't any such thing as a safe adolescent ward for a sixteen-year-old kid at Jefferson State Hospital. I'll leave the rest to your imagination. Take it away.

But to get back to the Birdman and his questions, one night Maxie, the adolescent ward's resident genius, explained this whole thing about the Birdman and our mothers to us.

A lot of evenings, after three or four of us adolescents had snuck off to smoke a joint, we'd come back to the main lounge and spread out on the sofas and chairs. The TV was always on and a few of the guys would actually watch it, but most of us just ignored it while we talked.

Maxie was always kind of like a judge holding court—he'd sit back in the big brown easy chair and stretch out his long skinny legs. He'd be wearing his black Led Zeppelin T-shirt and he'd have his long stringy hair pulled back in a ponytail. He always had a kind of sly grin on his face—a little one though, real subtle. He'd look like he was walking around laughing at his own private joke, especially when he was stoned. It made you want to know what he was thinking. It was kind of hard to tell just how old Maxie was, but you did get the feeling that he liked adolescence just fine and he planned to stay there permanently if he could.

One night in the lounge, Pinhead Richardson said, "Man, what is it with the Birdman? I mean, does he keep askin' you guys about your mother all the time?"

We all said, Yeah, what was his deal anyway?

Maxie folded his hands across his ribs and leaned his head back and closed his eyes. "It's Freud, man," he said.

"It's what, Maxie? Whaddaya mean?" Pinhead asked.

"Sigmund Freud, dumbshit. The original Birdman. German guy, died around fifty years ago or so."

"So what's some German guy got to do with my mom, Maxie?" Pinhead wanted to know.

"Yeah, that's what your dad wants to know," fat Decko piped in, cracking up like it was the most original joke anybody had ever made.

Maxie just stared at Decko for a minute like he couldn't believe he was sitting in the same room with him. Like he was seriously considering never letting Decko get high with him again. I loved how Maxie could do that with just a look.

He looked back to the rest of the group. "Sigmund Freud had this theory about the Oedipus complex. Basically, it means that deep down we all want to fuck our mothers and kill our fathers."

That got some reaction. "Jesus Christ," Pinhead said. "I mean, the Birdman's *seen* my mother. He's gotta know I've got no interest in fuckin' her."

Everybody nodded in agreement with that. "That's right, Maxie man. No way could somebody wanna fuck Pinhead's mother."

"No, no, no, you assholes. It's all unconscious. You don't *know* you wanna do it. You just do, deep down, where you don't recognize it."

"I do recognize wanting to kill my father, I gotta admit," Decko announced. He was trying to sound smart like Maxie, since making a joke didn't work.

"Why's it called Oedipus complex, Maxie?" I asked.

"It's named for Oedipus, this Greek guy. He actually did it."

That was lost on us; we just couldn't quite get what Maxie was saying. But of course no one ever wanted to admit it when they didn't understand something Maxie said. Finally, though, I just asked, "Did what, Maxie?"

"Fucked his mother, Rumer," he said, and he looked at me like he was challenging me or something.

"Whooaa . . ." Pinhead said, and he ended with a kind of sigh and then a whistle. "Why in the hell would you want *anybody* to know about something like that? I mean, why wouldn't you just keep it to yourself instead of naming a whole goddamn complex after yourself?"

Maxie was shaking his head. "Pinhead, you dumb, dumb, dumb-shit. *He* didn't name the thing, Sigmund Freud did. Oedipus was already dead when it happened."

"Well still, Maxie . . . shit, man . . ."

We all just shook our heads and whispered "Shit" under our breath until it sounded like an echo. What else can you say about a story like that?

But the truth is Miranda herself *is* a pretty interesting story. Sometimes I'd spend a whole session with the Birdman just telling him what I knew about her life. To begin with, she was too much like a little girl to think about her having sex at all. And too fat. By the time I was old enough to be thinking about those kinds of things, Miranda was just like a big fat little girl.

My dad called her Peter Pan sometimes because he said she wouldn't grow up. I could never figure out if that worked or not, though, because I thought Peter Pan was supposed to be a boy, but come to think of it I think a girl played Peter Pan in the movie on TV, maybe it *was* supposed to be a girl, but then why the name Peter? That was the thing about the adolescent ward, you could sit for hours trying to figure a thing like that out.

One time the Birdman asked me to tell him about Miranda, and I said, Well, what do you want to know, and he said, Well, what kinds of things did she do? I said, Well, one of the first things she did was to give me a girl's name.

"Yes," he said, getting all interested and excited (which always made me real uncomfortable). "I've wondered about your name, Rumer. Do you know why she named you that?"

"Because she read a story she liked by a writer named Rumer Godden. It was in a book she'd bought at the West Vernon Public

Library book sale. She went to that sale every year and bought about ten or fifteen books—they only charged five or ten cents a book. Most of the time she never read them, but the year she bought the Rumer Godden book she was pregnant with me, and I made her really uncomfortable so she couldn't sleep, so she pulled this Rumer Godden book out and read the whole thing one night."

"So she decided to name you Rumer because she liked the book?"

"That's right. She just assumed that since this person was a writer it must've been a man's name. But I had a teacher in third grade who asked me where I got my name and when I said I was named after a writer named Rumer Godden, this woman says to me, 'Well don't you know that Rumer Godden's a woman?'

"I went home and told Miranda that she'd named me after a woman and she said, 'I did? Well, I wouldn't worry about it, Rumer. That teacher's sure to be the only person in West Vernon who knows it's a woman and I'm sure she'll leave town soon.'

"And as a matter of fact she did. But for some reason I started telling everybody I knew that I had a girl's name. I'm not sure why I did it. I think maybe I wanted to tell everybody myself before they found out somehow behind my back."

As soon as I said that last part the Birdman started scribbling something down in his notebook, another thing he did that made me nervous.

Another time I told the Birdman about Miranda's doll collection. At that point, Miranda had 313 dolls. I knew because when she came to visit me once at Jefferson State, the first thing she told me was that she'd stopped off at an auction on her way and she'd found the prettiest antique doll—number 313—just like one her mother had had, she said. She got all flushed and excited just talking about it. "You want me to go out to the car and get it and bring it in for you to see?" she asked, but I told her no, that I thought I could wait till I got home.

The truth was, I hated Miranda's doll collection. When I was sixteen, I moved my bedroom out to the attic above the garage out back. I pulled an old space heater out of the basement and fixed it up to heat the attic in the winter, and I've slept out there for years, all so I can avoid the upstairs in my dad and Miranda's house.

All the neighbors assumed they'd kicked me out. But the fact is I moved out because of Miranda's doll collection.

She started collecting them a little after I was born. At first she kept them in her sewing room, on top of all the unpacked boxes and crates. But eventually the collection got too big, and she had to start keeping them out in the hallway. The summer before my brother Grant started high school, she got him to build shelves all along the walls in the upstairs hallway—five levels of them, from the floor to the ceiling, running along two long walls. By the time I was fourteen, those shelves were pretty much filled.

I hated walking along those walls crammed with dolls. At night when I'd be on my way to bed, I'd have to walk through that narrow space. I could feel all their creepy eyes on me, their hands reaching out in front of them. Sometimes one of their sleeves or one of their feet would rub alongside my back or my neck and I'd get the shivers all over and run for my room and slam my door. And then I'd hear Grant laughing at me. His room was at the other end of the hallway, right at the top of the stairs, which meant he never had to walk past the dolls at all.

She had every possible size, shape, and color of a doll up there. She would knit clothes for them—sweaters, capes, sometimes matching skirts and socks. Her life-size Sweet Sue doll was the first to greet you, right to your left at the top of the stairs, dressed in a pink and green sweater set with a matching hat that sat at an angle on top of her stiff blonde hair.

One shelf was all Barbie dolls. The space wasn't high enough for them to stand, so they all had to sit. The feet of the older ones—the ones with unbendable legs—stuck out over the edge of the shelf. A couple Barbies wore slinky lingerie outfits. Their tits looked like little plastic anthills. One time I stuck a paper clip inside Ken's pants to give him a hard-on and it was a couple weeks before Miranda even noticed.

Some of them looked like real babies. They wore white night-gowns and Miranda had them lying down with their eyes closed under pink and blue baby blankets. Those I didn't mind so much. They looked harmless and even kind of sweet. When I was younger I used to wish I could get them out of there, get them away from those other dolls.

Especially from the ones with the wide-open black eyes, the ones with fake eyelashes that looked like they were blinking at you and pouty little mouths that looked like they were laughing. Those were the dolls I hated the most, the ones that seemed to follow me with their eyes as I moved along the hall and reach out to grab me with their hard little fingers. What I could never understand was why, if they were supposed to be babies, whoever made them gave them the eyes and mouths of full-grown women. What were you supposed to do with a baby like that?

Then there were the dark-skinned ones. An Indian princess with black braids and a suede dress with fringe around the edge. And a black one with a long skirt that covered another head, this time a white one. You could flip the skirt one way or another, depending on whether you wanted a black doll or a white one. Miranda used to switch it back and forth every other week.

Those dark dolls bothered me, too, the way they stuck out and didn't fit in with all the other blonde-haired, rosy-cheeked ones. The Birdman said to me once, "Did you identify with them in some way?"

"No," I snapped back at him, "I did not. They're *dolls* for Christ's sake, pieces of plastic and wire and stuffing. Why would I identify with a goddamn piece of plastic?"

As soon as those words were out of my mouth I regretted them. He didn't say anything at all, and he wasn't writing anything in his notebook, either. He just looked at me with this look that said, "You tell me, Rumer. Why would you?"

I got to know that look right away. Whenever he gave it to me, I just stopped talking.

One time he said, "Why do you always call your mother by her first name? Why don't you call her Mom or Mother or something, like other people do?"

"Would you call a woman who's got three hundred dolls and wears pink babydoll pajamas in the middle of the day 'Mom'?" I asked him back. "I can just see it. I walk home from school and pour myself a glass of milk—does this fit what you've got in mind? I walk into the living room, where Miranda is sitting in front of the TV like always, knitting like always, with her frizzy yellow hair falling out of curlers all over her head like always. And I say, 'Hi, *Mom*, how was your day? What's that you're knitting, *Mother*, a new sweater for Sweet Sue? Some matching slippers for Barbie and Ken? Gee, *Mom*, we really should get you some new pajamas; I mean, that pink lace is all stained and torn, and you know, *Mother*, maybe you ought to comb your hair for once and hey, don't you think those short bloomers are kind of embarrassing, what with your flabby legs and all those varicose veins . . .'"

I stopped to take a breath and I noticed the way the Birdman was looking at me, with his thumb under his chin and his forefinger over his lips. For a minute it looked to me like he was almost wincing, like he really kind of wanted me to stop. I stared at him for just a second and then I said, "Would you call some forty-five-year-old Peter Pan in babydoll pajamas 'Mom'?"

Just to drive the point home. Just because I knew he'd already heard enough.

* * *

The dolls got up and walked into my room and watched me at night. They were all Miranda's real children and wanted to know what I was doing in her house.

Sweet Sue was the one they elected to speak for them. They all gathered around her and blinked their long black lashes at me while she talked. "We've taken a vote and we want you to get out of here. Grant can stay 'cause he's good-looking and people like him even though he's an arrogant son of a bitch. He's the only son Miranda wanted if she wanted any. She'd really rather just have us around, to tell the truth."

After that they'd reach out and grab at me when I walked by. They'd rustle their skirts and whisper about me behind my back. The Barbies would aim their stiff little feet at my eyes.

"Get out, Rumer. She never wanted you at all." But the black one and the Indian one would just look down at the floor, and the babies stayed under their blankets.

"You're not a girl and you're not really a boy. But you can't be one of us. Your skin is soft and hot and you've got parts to your body that we don't have. She doesn't want you, and your dad's too drunk to care."

I saw her kiss those dolls and comb their hair. Almost like she wanted to be one of them.

Flap, flap—those eyelashes would move up and down, like so many butterfly wings flapping just as I moved by. When I turned around they'd stop and hold real still, all of us holding our breath together. Then I'd race for the door.

Flap, flap.

Behind the noise of those flapping lashes, Grant was laughing. And Sweet Sue moved a couple steps closer to my door.

* * *

Miranda grew up on a farm over in Austin County. But her dad didn't own much land, and what land he did own was in what they called "bottoms," which meant it was right next to the river and flooded a lot of the time. They were pretty poor.

I didn't know my grandfather very well; he died when I was just a little thing. My grandmother died when I was twelve and she never said much to me before that. But I do remember her saying once, "What kinda name is Rumer? Biggest problem with that Miranda is that she reads too much. Got her into trouble in the first place."

I didn't know what she meant by that, of course, but I found out a few years later. One Thanksgiving day I was out working on my dad's old Plymouth and he walked out and started talking to me. He was drunk, as usual, but for some reason he was all sociable and talkative for a change, maybe because it was a holiday.

"You are a true Rutledge," he said to me. "Last of a dying line." And he laughed in a certain way he has, a way that lets you know he doesn't really think it's funny.

"What's that supposed to mean?" I asked him, keeping my head under the hood.

"Oh, just the way you're always workin' on that damn car or another one, always doin' somethin' with your hands. Your granddad was always tinkering with things—his old Model T or the printing press or some such thing.

"And as for me, I guess the thing I do well with my hands is pour!" Then that same laugh again.

"Well, you *used* to use your hands to write for the paper." I'd heard Miranda say this to him from time to time; truth was I could hardly remember the days when my dad was writing for the West Vernon *Ledger*.

"Yes, I did, Rumer. As I said, you're the end of a line. You could say I fell out of formation a long time ago."

"Well, Grant's makin' himself pretty famous around here. He's not doin' such a bad job of carrying on the Rutledge name." My brother Grant was a born-again preacher with a big following throughout the whole county. Not quite the same as running the newspaper maybe, but fame is fame, I figured.

Soon as I said that, though, my dad pulled my head out from under the hood.

"Listen, Rumer," he said. "There's no Rutledge blood in that boy. I want you to know that."

And that was when I got Roy Rutledge's story on who Miranda was.

"Your mother used to be a lively young woman, Rumer, hard as that may be for you to believe now."

"I know, I know. She had a twenty-inch waist and all kinds of boyfriends." Whenever anyone suggested to Miranda that she might want to try to lose some weight, she always told the story about how when she was eighteen years old she had a twenty-inch waist, as if that was supposed to make up for the size it was now.

"Well, she had a lot of boyfriends for a while, there. But when she got pregnant with Grant that was the end of that."

And even though I had a hard time taking it all in right then, at the same time I felt like a whole lot of things I'd never understood made damn clear sense all of a sudden.

Her parents had never really known what to do with her. But who would? Roy said; he shrugged and I shrugged back. They were older before they had her, and they were just simple farm folks. Apparently she took to reading all kinds of books when she was young and having all kinds of romantic fantasies, and they just could not control her. At least that's how my dad saw it.

After Grant was born she stayed on with them and they agreed to raise the baby and say it belonged to some cousin or somebody from Kentucky. Miranda started going to bars and putting on weight. But she kept on reading and having her fantasies, and that's when she first started her doll collection.

In the meantime, Roy had come back to West Vernon to settle in the old family house, which was still considered kind of a mansion back then. His father was dead and his older brother had been killed in the war, so it was left to him to run the West Vernon *Ledger*.

Roy couldn't fight in the war because of what he called a "weak heart." So he ended up staying behind and going to college. By the time he finished his dad had died. He went off to live in Cincinnati for a while then; I don't know much about what happened during that time. But then his mom got sick and he had to come back to this house to take care of her and that's when he took over the paper. And he just stayed on. Fallin' a little more out of formation each year.

He met Miranda in a bar over in Austin County. He'd been over there to cover a big high school basketball game for the paper, and afterward he went in the local bar to have a couple drinks before he went home. Miranda was there and he started talking to her, and the next thing he knew, he said, he was asking her to marry him.

"Most of the girls my age in West Vernon were already married," he told me, "and among the ones that weren't, none of them was any too interested in some newspaperman who hadn't even been in the war. I figured I'd need someone to help take care of this big old house, though, since my mother had died."

We both had to chuckle in that sarcastic way of his at that. Miranda, of course, has never been any too interested in taking care of the house.

Apparently Miranda thought it was kind of romantic to marry a newspaperman from two counties over, even if he hadn't been in the war. But she told him there was one condition. She had a one-year-old boy, she told him, and she would want to bring him along. And she would want my dad to give the boy his name.

"I thought that was kind of touching at the time, that she was so protective of that boy. It never occurred to me that he might be just another doll in her collection to her."

So Miranda married Roy Rutledge and came to live with him in the Rutledge house on Spring Street in West Vernon. He gave her boy Grant his name, and in another year or so I came along.

"So were you and her ever happy?" I asked him that day.

"I don't really recall, Rumer. I suppose we weren't all that unhappy anyway. But after you were born she kind of stayed more and more to herself. She started knitting things for those dolls of hers and it seemed like that and fussing over Grant were the only things she ever cared about. She never paid much mind to you, as you know."

I just stared at him then. If he'd noticed that, why hadn't he done anything about it? I guess that's when I started to get mad. Up till that point I guess he hadn't really said anything that got to me. But that did.

Then it seemed like maybe he was reading my mind, because he said, "You know, Rumer, part of why I just leave you alone most of the time is that I wish my parents had done that to me. If I hadn't had it drilled in my head over and over that I had a responsibility to my family and this town, that I had to come back here and run that goddamn paper, I'd have stayed on in Cincinnati. And I wish to hell I'd done that. I wish I'd stayed right there."

His hands were shaking and he was reaching for the flask of whiskey that he always kept in his shirt pocket. And right then I just hated him. I thought he didn't just have a weak heart, he had a weak everything. Everything about him was weak and useless, and he'd never given me a goddamn single, solitary thing.

And I think I hated him the most because I figured I would end up just like him, only worse, because there wasn't much left to being a Rutledge anymore. The house was falling apart and looked more like some kind of freak-show haunted house than any kind of family mansion. The paper was being taken away from him piece by piece and there was hardly any money left and none coming in, and he was too drunk ninety-nine percent of the time to give a damn.

I guess it was during that talk that I decided I'd have to find a way to fend for myself. Grant was a high school hero and I knew he'd probably go to college on a football scholarship and then come back and coach or something. But I'd already figured out that I didn't really fit in, and it was gonna be harder for me to find a way to get on in West Vernon.

I could fix cars, though, so a year or two after that I started doing it for some extra cash at Jess Langley's filling station. And around the same time I met my buddy Jim Eiseley, and I started sellin' grass.

So I guess it was that talk that got me started in life in a way. I kind of regret the way it turned out now. The talk I mean. It seemed like after that day Roy and I could never just have a normal conversation without ending up yelling at each other.

I guess I should've kept quiet, but after I heard him say, "I should've stayed in Cincinnati," I just couldn't stop myself. "Well, I wish to hell you'd stayed there, too," I said. "Maybe then I wouldn't've been born to live in this rundown trap with a crazy old woman and a drunk." And then I just went back to work on the Plymouth.

Come to think of it, he didn't yell back that time. He just went back into the house, kind of slow and shaky like an old man. I watched him out of the corner of my eye, and I remember thinking, He looks like an old, old man already.

So anyway, as I said, I don't know much about Miranda's parents, just that they were old and seemed like they didn't really understand who she was. I do remember, though, that we had good meals when we went out to my grandmother's house on Sundays. Miranda mostly made Campbell's soup and macaroni and cheese when we were home.

It seemed like instead of growing up as she got older she grew *down* or something—like she just became more and more like a kid. When I was little I remember she did some fairly normal things for a mom—took us to Cub Scouts and to our grandparents' house, bought us new sneakers and blue jeans, took us to get our hair cut.

And here's something else I remember. Sometimes Roy would go away for a week or two, I don't know where; they always said "a conference" but even when I was a kid I think I just assumed that meant a bender. He couldn't get by with a serious one in West Vernon, or at least not back then, when we were little. I guess then he cared enough what people thought to try not to make his drinking quite that obvious.

But wherever he went we didn't really care. Because when he was gone, Miranda really came to life. She was younger and still kind of pretty then. I wouldn't say she had a twenty-inch waist, but then I would say she probably never did (and who'd want one anyway, I always wanted to know—you'd look like a goddamn starvation victim on TV). Keep in mind this was a long time ago, and I don't remember it very well. But I know we used to drive Roy to the train station (now you can't even get a train anywhere less than a hundred miles from here), and then the three of us, Miranda and Grant and me, would go out for lunch somewhere.

She'd be all dressed up with lipstick on, and happy, too, and she'd tell us to order whatever we wanted. So I'd have a hamburger and french fries and an ice cream soda, and Grant would order those things too, but he never seemed to be enjoying himself. Sometimes then she'd take us to our grandparents' house, and then she might go off for a few days herself.

I don't know where she went. To tell you the truth I never really cared. But Grant did. He'd sulk around and snarl at anybody that tried to talk to him, my grandparents included. So I'd just steer clear of him, which I didn't mind doing. I always liked being on that farm, even if it was run down. And the more I was there, the more I got to putting together my *own* story about who Miranda was.

* * *

Her parents' house was a square white box. The old woman hardly ever moved off the rocking chair on the front porch, and the old man limped along the fence row and picked up used cans for the tin.

Inside the floors sloped and the linoleum arched up like a hunchback. Wood burned in the kitchen stove and the cold dirt smell of the cellar was there just below the smell of the last meal the old woman had cooked.

And then there was Miranda's room. Just the way she left it, with a lacy pink bedspread on the bed. In the top dresser drawer was all her old make-up: caked-dry rouge the color of candy apples, lipstick tubes stained on the sides like blood, the powder case with a cracked gray mirror stuck in the back, leaving a layer of pink dust all over the bottom of the drawer.

She would sit there with her twenty-inch waist and paint on babydoll cheeks and lips, then put a layer of pink powder over all of it. Later a baby screamed in a basket in the corner and she had a wider waist and she painted herself bright red. Over and over those fat babydoll lips, redder and redder, and she'd smile in the mirror at her red lips and red teeth and red eyes. A baby screamed in the corner of her room; why was he always screaming, she probably thought. She'd have to make him a bottle, feed him something sweet—he'd be quiet then like a little doll.

But outside there was nothing but low, flat fields. Miles and miles of corn turning brown in the sun. Nothing for her but a job in a factory or another farmhouse kitchen, frying bacon and eggs for some fat farmer with dirty nails and a big old belly. No words, nothing pretty, nothing shiny, no fancy car or lace curtains. She would paint herself redder and redder and pick up a book to read.

On the back row of her room there were two bookshelves full of them. They came each month in the mail from somewhere out east, my grandmother said. Skinny, flimsy things with cheap white cardboard covers and pictures of women with tiny waists and big breasts, old-fashioned lace dresses, fear in their sleepy eyes. Fear like she thought she wanted to have. Fear of some dark thing, some big, dark, dangerous thing, lurking around some corner out there.

Lurking behind a circus tent, carrying a big black camera bag. He wouldn't even take her in his car, he'd take her off across Carroll Creek, into the woods behind the fairgrounds. He'd put down some kind of satiny thing that he hung behind the people he took pictures of, put that down on the wet ground. And maybe her yellow-blonde hair got messed up and her lipstick was all smeared and she didn't look like anything more than a little girl, but by that time he wouldn't care, he'd just have a go at her anyway. And she'd see what that big dark thing around the corner was and why those women's eyes were so afraid. And maybe she'd wonder why they wanted to be scared like that, wonder what all the fuss was for, feel cold and dirty and wish she was back under her pink lace bedspread with a book that made it all sound so much better than it really was.

Only a little later she'd be fatter and so much older, with a baby crying in the corner. Only two reasons to leave that room and that fat little baby boy at all: to go to her job in the factory, and to go out to the bars at night to drink with the other used-up men and women. Used up already, even though she wasn't any more than a little girl. Maybe she felt as old as all of them, and maybe all of them were old before their time and just knew way too much. Maybe they were there because they knew that all that was out there was miles and miles of cornfields and factory jobs and farmers' kitchens in little square houses and the smell of the cellar and the cold, wet ground.

* * *

It's funny how some stories get started. The truth was, while I might have knocked on some of those women's doors, I never once pulled out any private piece of my anatomy when somebody answered.

But for some reason I never much minded the fact that people thought I did. I kind of liked it, to tell the truth.

And now I guess I know that the Birdman probably knew that all along, and that's what I was doing at age twenty-one on the adolescent ward at Jefferson State Hospital, hiding from all the eyes and ears and mouths in West Vernon, Indiana, and telling stories about Miranda, a Peter Pan if there ever was one, there on the porch in her babydoll pajamas and long past giving a damn about any of those West Vernon eyes or ears or mouths.

4. Slipstream

She is shedding language, filling her house with bone and rock.

More leaking than shedding, really. Losing it quickly, almost from the pores. At a conference recently she paused in the midst of delivering a paper, glasses sliding down her nose. It was a moment that in the past would have evoked pure panic, but this time it was lovely to her. What was she going to say? The odd black shapes on the white sheet before her offered no clue. But what did it really matter? The sea of faces before her, the heat of her own flushed face were suddenly beautiful and strange. In a way no words could ever say anyway. She walked away from the podium.

It's not a sad old story about some poor woman going gradually senile—poor us, a shame what happens when we age.

It's not a sad old story at all.

Not sad because she is smiling and laughing most of the time. She is a professor of language and literature, and for years she has read and heard and written about the folly of our vain attempts to master language. But she never quite understood that folly until now.

When she walked out of the hotel into the hot Phoenix sun she smelled something airy and fine and thought immediately, Jacaranda.

Now there's a graceful word. Jacaranda. *What does it matter what she really smelled?*

Not sad because she sits now with an open book on her lap and forgets what it's there for. She walks to the river bank and fills her lap, her pockets, any space she can find with rocks. Basalt, granite, slate, pumice, mica. *Her tongue slaps their surfaces like water.*

What was she reading? Where is that book? What does it matter?

Not old because she isn't, not really. Quite a few years away from retirement. Ten years married to an actor who's long gone now, two unsatisfying affairs after that. No particular interest in women, though she did try once. Children grown and gone to cities south of her. What she had left was work—her relationship with the English language. But now the words are leaking from her skin.

She is almost like a girl again.

In the evenings a teenage couple, boy and girl, run by her house in their jogging shorts. For a week she watched until one night she put on shorts of her own and followed when they ran by. They looked back once or twice, laughing. "Come on, hurry up," they said.

She does. She keeps up. She's riding in their wake, she thinks, and this one came to her like birdsong: Slipstream.

Each night now she does this. She is not old. Not old because when they run by marshes she hears the sound and knows immediately. Tree frogs.

What the tree frogs do is better than most singing she has heard.

In some rocks from the river she finds fossils. Prehistoric life, or at least something older than she is. Rubbing her finger against those crevices she smells dust and bone. Now that is old. It's true that she may die but even then she will be far from old. When she runs behind the teenagers her body smells like youth to her. Sweating, sour, and lovely. Far from old.

And not a story because for once she isn't looking for one. She'd just like to feel her face flush hot like that again, feel that blazing southwestern sun, without having to step up to a podium to do it. Words are monstrous unless they appear, like magic, from somewhere else, she has decided. Jacaranda. Basalt. Slipstream.

When the teenage couple finish jogging they always smoke a joint. Once they offered her some but she refused. She simply stands nearby and inhales deeply. Sensimilla. *It reminds her of her son.*

And then somehow she finds her way back home. Smelling herself. The only word she thinks is Me. Me, *all the way back. Back to somewhere, though she's forgotten where.*

University Press of New England

publishes books under its own imprint and is the publisher for Brandeis University Press, Dartmouth College, Middlebury College Press, University of New Hampshire, Tufts University, and Wesleyan University Press.

About the Author

Joyce Hinnefeld's short stories and nonfiction have appeared in magazines, journals, and the anthologies *Prairie Hearts: Women's Writings on the Midwest* (Outrider Press, 1996) and *Many Lights in Many Windows: Twenty Years of Great Fiction and Poetry from the Writers Community* (Milkweed Editions, 1997). She teaches at Moravian College in Bethlehem, Pennsylvania.

Library of Congress Cataloging-in-Publication Data

Hinnefeld, Joyce.
Tell me everything and other stories / Joyce Hinnefeld.
p. cm.
"A Middlebury / Bread Loaf book."
1997 Katharine Bakeless Nason Literary Publication Prize.
ISBN 0-87451-875-X (cloth : alk. paper)
I. Title.
PS3558.I5448T4 1998
813'.54—dc21 98-13291